HIS BEAUTIFUL SWAN

Lydia was about to follow her hostess when Evan called to her. "A moment, please," he said, joining her at the foot of the stairs. "There is something I should like to say to you."

"Please, Evan, if you must read me a lecture, can it not wait until tomorrow?"

"No such reading was in my plans, but what I have to say can wait, if you insist."

She shook her head. "No, I do not insist. I will hear whatever is on your mind."

"It is about you," he said. "I know you love Sebastian, and since you have not asked my opinion of him, I will say nothing on that subject. But I pray you do not change who you are for him. Or for any man. If a man truly loves you, he will love all of you. Just as you are."

"Just as I am? Bones and all?"

Evan caught her hand and held it between both of his, his warmth and his strength acting like a magnet, tugging at Lydia and making her wish she dared step just that little bit closer—close enough that he might be tempted to wrap his arms around her and hold her close. Hold her just for a minute.

"Believe me," he said softly. "To the right man, those bones will be infinitely precious."

At his whispered words, all the embarrassment and disappointment Lydia had suffered that evening seemed to fade into nothingness, like a bad dream dispelled by the light. "How can you be so certain?"

"Because," he said, "I am a man, and *I* would not wish you to be anyone but who you are. . . ."

Books by Martha Kirkland

THE GALLANT GAMBLER
THREE FOR BRIGHTON
THE NOBLE NEPHEW
THE SEDUCTIVE SPY
A GENTLEMAN'S DECEPTION
THAT SCANDALOUS HEIRESS
HIS LORDSHIP'S SWAN

Published by Zebra Books

HIS LORDSHIP'S SWAN

Martha Kirkland

ZEBRA BOOKS
Kensington Publishing Corp.
http://www.zebrabooks.com

To my editor, John Scognamiglio, with appreciation for his continued faith in my writing.

Prologue

"And did none of them offer us the least hope for the lad?" Evan Trent asked.

His mother shook her head. Her lavender silk bonnet still reposed on her salt-and-pepper hair, for she had been too concerned with her report to think of removing either her bonnet or the matching traveling cloak. "We have now seen every physician, every surgeon, and every quack from Liverpool to London, and to a man they are agreed that my nephew will never hear again. Though his health is totally regained, the young being so resilient, the fever had a devastating and permanent effect upon his hearing."

Tears sparkled in Lady Trent's dark eyes—eyes so like her son's. "On one physician's recommendation, I purchased a hearing trumpet, but I regretted it immediately. Young Jack did not react at all well to the sight of such an instrument."

"Tossed it out the window, did he?"

"No. I only wish he had done so."

Lady Trent brushed aside the tears that threatened to spill down her delicately powdered cheeks. "The lad vowed he would rather die than use an old man's aid; then he sank into a state of depression. He is in it still, and nothing I have said or done these past two days has had the power to rouse him from that despondency."

Evan took his mother's hand in his. "Do not blame yourself, ma'am. Jack is thirteen years old, and just coming into the most difficult period in a youngster's development. This could not have happened at a worse time."

"Can there ever be a *good* time to lose one's hearing?"

When Evan muttered something beneath his breath, his mother begged his pardon. "I should not take my frustration out on you."

"If not me, then who? After weeks of travel and disappointment, you have a right to be frustrated."

"I confess I am at my wits' end. Your cousin has taken to carrying a writing pad and pencil with him at all times, and with each day that passes, he is becoming more reticent to speak in front of strangers. Because he can no longer hear his own voice, he is afraid his speech will begin to sound strange, and that he will become a figure of fun."

George Evan Philip Trent, the sixth Viscount Trent, muttered an obscenity. Before he could apologize for the slip, however, her ladyship continued. "I may as well tell you the rest of the story."

"There is more?"

"One final but most important thing remains. Just before our chaise pulled into the carriageway a few minutes ago, my nephew informed me that he had come to a decision. He vows he will never marry."

"That is the depression talking, ma'am. Jack has only just begun to notice females, and considering his tender age, I think it is early days for such a decision. Do not be concerned, for—"

"But I *am* concerned," Lady Trent continued, "and so must you be. For Jack bid me most emphatically to inform you that he no longer wishes to be regarded as the heir presumptive."

"What!"

"Your cousin says that if you have any regard for him at all, you will relieve him of that obligation."

"But—"

"He wants your promise, Evan, that you will begin immediately to search for a suitable bride for yourself, so that *your* child will be the future viscount."

Evan had remained for some minutes beside his mother on the rose brocade settee in the sitting room adjoining her bedchamber. Now, no longer able to sit still, he stood and strode across to the window that looked out upon the Italian-style terraces that worked their way down to the shallow tributary of the Mersey River. The sun had begun to set, and the gold and orange of the sky was reflected in the gently flowing waters. At the water's edge, numerous water fowl, among them the great crested grebes, with their bright red and brown heads and their pure-white breasts, floated about quietly in groups of six or eight, as if not yet ready to call it a day.

"A suitable bride," Evan said, the words all but sticking in his throat. "And if I do not wish to give such a promise?"

"Then I fear my nephew may slip further and further into this present depression."

Lady Trent said no more for several minutes, waiting until her son turned back to her, so that she could look into his face. Evan possessed thick, slightly wavy dark hair, and by this time of day, a slight shadow always showed on his square jawline and his determined chin. As well, even after five years home from the Royal Navy, his skin still possessed the swarthy look of the sailor. A small scar bisected his left eyebrow—a memento from the Battle of Trafalgar—and to any who did not know Evan, and love him as she did, he appeared a rather formidable man. For that reason, there were few who were brave enough to tell him something he did not wish to hear.

"Will it be so bad?" she asked. "You are a handsome, wealthy peer. Finding a suitable wife should prove no problem."

"The problem, ma'am, is that I do not wish to marry."

He returned to his contemplation of the grebes upon the river, where one bird struggled beneath the weight of her fully matured offspring, which still insisted upon hitching a ride on her back. In sympathy with the mother bird, who could not rid herself of her family obligations, Evan said, "I had always pinned my hopes on young Jack marrying and securing the line. With an heir presumptive, I felt I could take my time. I could marry if I chose, or remain a bachelor for life if it pleased me to do so."

"Unfortunately," Lady Trent said, "you no longer have that luxury. Nor, I must add, have you time to ponder the matter over long. You were thirty last Christmas, my love, and even a viscount cannot wait forever to choose a wife. In time, one's choices become limited."

Evan elected not to disabuse her ladyship of that rather naive belief. Though the primary reason he had turned his face against marriage was the example set him by his father, who was a dismal failure as a husband, a secondary reason for Evan's wish to remain single was the all too nauseating willingness of the young ladies of society to throw themselves at his head. Let Lady Trent call him handsome—it was the prerogative of mothers to think their children were filled with every virtue and possessed of remarkably good looks—but Evan did not rate his looks above average.

Not that it mattered. Had Evan been twice his age, toothless, and covered in warts, there would still be young ladies by the dozens happy to share his title, his wealth, and if need be his bed.

For that very reason, Evan did not think an inability to hear would limit his cousin Jack's marital opportunities, not once it was known that the lad would inherit his cousin's title and estates. However, Jack was of a different opinion, and at the moment, the boy had enough to do just coming to grips with this trauma. His recent illness, plus the shock of losing his hearing, were stressful enough for any thirteen-year-old; he did not need the added pressure of thinking he must fulfill his duty to the family.

"Damnation," Evan muttered. He said nothing more for several moments; then, with a sigh, he said, "So be it."

Rightly interpreting the resignation in her son's voice, Lady Trent interrupted his contemplation of the floating fowl. "I knew I might depend upon you, dear boy. Now, it remains only for you to choose a likely female."

"Actually, the grebes have put me in mind of someone."

His mother smiled for the first time since her son had entered the sitting room. "Well, this is progress indeed. You say the grebes brought the young lady to mind. Is she, like the birds, a redhead?"

"Heaven forbid! You know what such females are like. They believe their hair color entitles them to behave like termagants, and the last thing I want is a lifetime filled with Cheltenham dramas. If I must marry, let it be to someone serene, one not given to flights of fancy and fits of temper."

Though his mother was of the opinion that a girl with a bit of a temper might be just what Evan needed, she knew better than to meddle too far in her son's affairs. Getting right to the point, she said, "A blonde, then. Do I know the young lady?"

"Ladies, ma'am. In the plural. And yes, you met them in Bath when we were there this past spring."

"Them! My boy, I assure you, one wife will suffice. Besides, though I have never researched the matter, I am persuaded there are laws in this country prohibiting polygyny."

Evan returned to the settee and sat beside his mother. "I refer to the twins we met at the Thompsons' cotillion. Diamonds of the first water; both of them beautiful blue-eyed blondes. But you may rest assured, I mean to ask for only one of them."

"You cannot know how relieved I am to hear it."

Evan chuckled. "If I remember correctly, their surname was Swann."

"Of course. Now I see the connection to the

grebes. And you are correct, my boy, their names were Clarissanne and Clorinda Swann. Or was it Clothilda?"

She looked to her son for confirmation, but he merely shrugged his broad shoulders. "It was something outlandish like that. I never bothered to learn their first names. What was the point? For the life of me, I could never tell the young ladies apart."

"You could—" His mother looked at him as if he had grown a second head. "Evan, are you telling me that you have not a *preference* for one over the other?"

"A preference? How could I? I did not speak to either one of them above five minutes. Besides, they are mirror images. They are blessed with identically lovely faces; they possess the same rather quiet personalities; and if you can tell me that one of those perfect figures weighs as much as an ounce more than the other, I will say it cannot be."

When his mother spoke, her voice was none too steady. "The young ladies were lovely in both face and form, and well-behaved besides. Which explains why they were so vastly popular at all the parties and concerts. I cannot remember ever seeing them without at least a dozen admirers in their wake."

"As you say, ma'am. The Swann twins were perfection itself. Ergo, they are perfect for my needs. Beautiful, reasonably intelligent, well-bred, and quiet. And one has only to look at their mother, who is still a handsome woman, to see that the daughters should age well. Furthermore, their home is within an easy day's travel. What more could one ask of a future bride?"

"What more, indeed?" Lady Trent stared at her

son for several moments. "I suppose a mother might be forgiven for hoping that her only son would find *love* in his marriage."

Choosing not to hear that comment, Evan said, "I have it on good authority that their father's estate is mortgaged to the hilt and that Sir Beecham sent the twins to Bath in hopes of their snagging rich husbands—husbands who would be willing to replenish the family coffers. Since the town seemed filled to overflowing with fortune hunters and half-pay officers, this should work in my favor. I can certainly afford to part with a reasonable amount to pay the baronet's debts, and his greed should simplify the entire courtship process."

"Simplify it for whom?" Obviously not sharing her son's cavalier outlook, Lady Trent said, "I can think of at least one complication. Sooner or later you will be obliged to ask the man for his daughter's hand. Call me overly nice in my notions, but I think a father—even a greedy one—would expect a perspective son-in-law to know the girl's name."

Evan waved the caveat aside. "That can be gotten around easily enough. I need only write and ask the fellow if I might call upon him, my purpose to propose marriage to Miss Swann."

Evan reached inside his coat and extracted his lucky gold sovereign, balancing it on his forefinger prior to flipping it. "You may call it, ma'am." When she declined the honor, he said, "As you wish. Heads I ask him for the younger twin. Tails I ask for the older one. Their father will supply the correct name when he answers my letter."

"But, my boy, I cannot like—"

Mary Trent said no more, for her son had flipped

the coin and allowed it to fall to the muted rose-and-green carpet, and now he was checking the results of his toss. "Tails," he said, retrieving the coin. "It is settled, then. I will ask Lord Swann if I might have the hand of his *eldest* daughter."

One

"Marry Lord Trent? Really, Papa, this is too preposterous. I do not even *know* the man."

Miss Lydia Elizabeth Swann stared at the single sheet of vellum her father had given her to read. True enough, the letter writer had asked for the hand of *Miss Swann,* Sir Beecham's *eldest* daughter, and that was Lydia, but even though she had read through the politely couched words twice, she still did not understand them. "I tell you again, Papa, I have no knowledge of anyone named Trent. Viscount or no, I never met him, so how could he possibly remember me with fondness?"

"But he says he met you," her father insisted.

"And I say it is not possible. Except for that time eight years ago when we all went to Aunt Minerva's wedding in Yorkshire, I have never been farther from Lower Dewes than Newcastle-under-Lyme, and that village boasts nothing that passes for upper rooms. To attend such a ball as Lord Trent mentions, one would have to be in London, or at one of the fashionable spa towns."

"Nevertheless, the viscount insists that—"

"Bath!" Lydia snapped her fingers, happy to have solved the riddle. "Lord Trent must have met the twins this past spring when they visited Bath. Do you not see, Papa? This proposal is meant for Clarissanne, who is the older twin."

Sir Beecham Swann did not care a fig where the viscount had made his daughter's acquaintance, or even *which* daughter. All he could think of was the marriage settlement such an alliance would bring. "Never met this Lord Trent," he said. "Don't travel in such exalted circles. But rumor has it that when the present viscount's father turned up his toes about fifteen or sixteen months ago, he left the estates in prime order and his only heir well greased with lard."

Lydia's papa was not known for taking any real interest in conversations that did not include the finer points of hunting dogs, or the weight, length, and duplicity of some wide-mouthed bass, and his daughter felt certain that time was running out in which to secure the baronet's attention. Hoping to make her point before he quit the subject, she said, "If you will recall, Papa, I did not go to Bath. Only my mother and the twins, Clarissanne and Clorinda, made the trip."

"And a fine lot of good it did us!" Sir Beecham said, warming to a familiar theme. His face grew almost as red as his carrot-colored hair. "Might have known that hound would not hunt. A waste of good money sending the twins to Bath. I was assured they would find rich husbands, but nothing could have been farther from the truth."

"But, Papa, they—"

"One came home engaged to a purse-pinched curate," he said, his tone filled with disgust, "and t'other returned besotted with a half-pay officer with nothing to recommend him but a pretty uniform and a ready smile."

Though Lydia had heard this lament many times these past three months, she held her peace, allowing her father to give vent to his disappointment. "Girls with their looks!" he said. "I tell you, Lydia. It is just another example of the cruel tricks fate plays on me again and again."

Though he railed loudly enough, Lydia listened with only half her attention, for she knew two things to be true: First, that her father had not expended even a groat to send his daughters to the spa town, and second, that Sir Beecham would soon forget all about the Bath fiasco.

Convinced that worry was a complete waste of time, the baronet's philosophy consisted of one basic belief, that he would always "come about." His days were spent riding to hounds, fowling, fishing, and generally throwing good money after bad. Whether it was foolish wagers, or purchasing a bag of bones masquerading as a horse, or trading for a hound that continually lost the scent, Beecham Swann seemed completely unable to live within the modest means derived from the rents of the Swannleigh estate.

If he had ever given a thought to what might become of his wife and three daughters once he put his spoon in the wall, such concern would come as a severe shock to those who knew him best. In fact, the twins owed their trip to Bath to a chance comment by one of their father's hunting cronies.

"Too bad," the fellow had said, "that Cleo and

what's her name cannot go up to town for a season. Fine-looking girls, both of them. You'd have only to turn them loose for a party or two, and sure as Bob's your uncle, they would come home betrothed to wealthy young men."

Of course, a London season had been out of the question, and though Sir Beecham lamented the money spent on the Bath trip, the funds had not come from his pockets—it being mathematically impossible to take something from nothing. Actually, Lady Swann's mother had been so good as to frank her daughter and all three of her granddaughters to a month in the fashionable watering hole.

Unfortunately, Lydia did not get to accompany her mother and her sisters. Not that she had anyone but herself to blame for that! After all, who but Lydia would confront a polecat half an hour before time for the coach to leave?

She had just stepped down the lane to tell old Granny Watkins good-bye, and on the walk home, Lydia had met the wretched polecat. The weasel-like creature had come from the direction of the poultry house, with the telltale yellow of egg yolks still staining his face. It was a toss-up as to which of them was more startled by the encounter, Lydia or the furry egg thief, but the polecat had had the final word!

Before Lydia could turn and run, the creature raised its tail and sprayed her from head to toe.

The odor was unbelievably repugnant, and because the tear-inducing stench that clung to the unfortunate victim's skin and hair made even Lydia nauseous, she could readily understand the reticence of her mother and her sisters to travel with her for eight hours in a closed carriage. So it was that Lydia remained at home while her sisters went to Bath, her one opportunity to meet eligible young men and possibly contract a suitable alliance gone in a puff of polecat spray.

Not that Lydia would have made the spa town sit up and take notice, not in the manner the twins had done. Lydia Swann was by no means an antidote, but she resembled her father's side of the family. A bit on the tall side, she had been cursed with coppery red hair and the inescapable sprinkle of freckles across a rather pert nose. Still, a female with twice her looks would have suffered by comparison with the divinely fair Clarissanne and Clorinda.

Because no one outside the family could distinguish Clarissanne from Clorinda, the twins were known in the village simply as "the Swans." Since there were three sisters, some would-be wit had dubbed them, "the Swans and the Ugly Duckling," and to Lydia's dismay, the sobriquets had taken hold.

Not that Lydia was disliked in the neighborhood. Far from it! She was generally held to be the most personable of the trio, and had there been an eligible young man in the village, and had his fate been put to a general vote, everyone would have chosen Lydia as the fortunate gentleman's fiancée.

As luck would have it, no such eligible young man existed. Except for Sebastian Osborne, the dashing young man whose father had married her aunt, Minerva, the widow of one of Lydia's mother's brothers, there never had been anyone for the girls to fall in love with. Naturally, when the Swanns attended the wedding, some eight years back, and the sisters clapped eyes on the handsome Sebastian, all three girls had fallen head over heels for their aunt's new stepson.

Lydia being the oldest, she had fallen the hardest. At sixteen, she had fancied herself in love for life, and when the Swanns had returned to their home after the wedding celebration, Lydia had cried for weeks on end, her heart and her mind filled with memories of the young Adonis, astride his white horse.

"*I* know him," her father said.

"Sebastian?" Lydia asked, somewhat dazed by the rude interruption of her recollections of the blue-eyed god who figured as her ideal man.

"Trent," her father replied. "Pay attention, my girl."

"Of course, Papa. How foolish of me. You were saying you are acquainted with Lord Trent."

"Not him, actually. It was his father I knew, though ours was only a nodding acquaintance. Rich as Croesus, the previous viscount. Had the devil's own luck at cards. Never seemed to lose. And as I remember, he also had quite a way with the lady-birds. Once had two barques of frailty in his keeping at the same—"

Suddenly recalling to whom he spoke, Sir Beecham pretended a bout of coughing.

Lydia ignored both the information about the previous viscount and her father's attempt to cover his faux pas. She was much more interested in see-ing the end to this misunderstanding. "When you answer the letter, Papa, I beg you will inform his lordship in no uncertain terms that it is Clarissanne he is remembering, and not me. And be certain you inform him that Clarissanne has been engaged since April."

"Answered the letter more than a sennight ago," her father replied. "Sent word that very day."

Lydia looked once again at the letter in her hand, only then noticing that the date on the missive was twelve days past. "And?" she said, something in her father's stubborn stance making her uneasy, "what did you tell him?"

"Told him to come take his mutton with us as soon as he wished."

"But, Papa, both the twins are spoken for."

"Deuce take it, Daughter! Have your wits gone begging? Lord Trent did not ask for one of the twins. You saw for yourself what he wrote. He asked for my eldest."

"Papa, this is foolish beyond permission. He will take one look at me and—"

"Give you his betrothal ring," Sir Beecham said. "As a gentleman, he can do nothing else, for he has asked for your hand and I have given my permission."

"Well, I have not given mine! You seem to have forgotten, Papa, that I have turned four-and-twenty. No longer a minor, I can decide for myself what is best for me to do."

"While you live under my roof," her father said, his tone as serious as Lydia had ever heard it, "you will do as I say."

"Surely you cannot—"

"Lord Trent will be here any day now to make you a formal offer of marriage, and I warn you, Lydia, I will not tolerate any female foolishness. When he proposes, I expect you to accept."

"But, Papa, I—"

"You heard me! And make no mistake about it. Before this week is out, you *will* be engaged to Lord Trent."

" 'Course I know Sir Beecham," the blacksmith said. "Grew up here in Lower Dewes, him and me both. That where you be bound? Swannleigh Manor?"

Evan Trent paused just outside the blacksmith's shop. He did not make a practice of eavesdropping, but the moment he heard the baronet's name, he gave his full attention to the smith, who was in conversation with Evan's coachman. They had stopped in the small village because one of the coach horses had thrown a shoe, and while they waited for the blacksmith to see to the animal, Evan had strolled over to the small inn for a tankard of ale. Upon his return to the smithy's, he heard the two men in conversation.

"Swannleigh Manor," his coachman repeated, "that be the place right enough. You say you know the family?"

"Since I were a lad. And his lordship's father afore him. Been Swanns at Lower Dewes for near two hundred years."

The powerful man in the leather apron swung a heavy sledgehammer, hitting the red-hot horseshoe he held between long, iron tongs. He did not resume his conversation until the shoe was beaten into shape and the still-hot metal had been dipped into a bucket of water, causing the water to sizzle and steam to rise into the air. Above the sizzling noise, he said, "Don't know what'll become of the place when Sir Beecham turns up his toes."

"How's that?" the coachman asked.

"No sons." The smith whispered that bit of information, as though it might be thought a slur on the baronet. "Just the three daughters."

Three? For the life of him, Evan could not remember meeting any but the twins. The third daughter must not have accompanied her sisters to Bath. The twins were no more than twenty, probably the other sister was still a schoolroom chit.

"There's Miss Lydia Swann," the smith continued. "She's the oldest by about four years—"

The oldest!

Evan experienced an upsurge in the uneasiness that had gnawed at his insides for the past two weeks. From the moment he had posted his letter to Sir Beecham, the normally cautious Evan had been calling himself an idiot for putting his proposal on paper. As for not discovering the girl's name before making his offer, only a cretin would have committed that folly.

Hoping he had not heard the smithy correctly, Evan reached inside his coat and removed the baronet's letter, which had arrived by return post. While he read the single sheet for perhaps the hundredth time, his earlier misgivings were joined by a frisson of suspicion.

In his missive, Sir Beecham had neglected to supply the name of the appropriate twin, and at the first reading, Evan had been disappointed to discover the omission. Now, in light of this latest information, the prospective bridegroom read with clearer eyes, noting that the young lady's father had

taken pains to answer in the sketchiest of terms that
his eldest daughter would be pleased to receive the
viscount's flattering proposal. *His eldest.*

"Then there's the twins," the smithy added.
"Can't get my tongue around their outlandish
names. Not that it matters, for there's none in the
village can tell the twins one from t'other." He began to chuckle. " Round here, the three misses are
known as 'The Swans and the Ugly Duckling.' "

The Ugly Duckling!

" 'Course, Miss Lydia don't pay us no mind. But
then she's the nicest sort of young lady, never too
starched up to enjoy a bit of fun."

Evan heard no more, for something resembling a
giant hand had reached inside his stomach and begun to twist his entrails first one way, then the other.
"Heaven help me," he muttered. "What have I
done?"

For the next half hour, that question echoed in
his head, along with the growing conviction that he
had been made a fool of. He had treated the business of the proposal in a careless, slapdash manner,
and he had no one but himself to blame if there
was a mix-up. Still, Sir Beecham must have known
that Evan had offered for one of the twins, and not
the duckling. Why would he offer for this Lydia person, when he had no knowledge of her existence?

The answer was simple: he had not done so, and
Lord Swann knew it!

Unfortunately, it was too late for Evan to take himself to task, and far too late to question Sir
Beecham's motives. The man was pressed for money,
and he had a daughter so homely she had been left
on the shelf. What more was there to say? All that

remained to be discovered was how much it would cost Evan to extricate himself from this debacle.

He had only just asked himself that question when the coachman turned the horses in at the wrought-iron gates of Swannleigh Manor and continued up the badly rutted carriageway. After being tossed about like a ship on a stormy sea, the coach came to a stop outside a once-handsome gray stone manor house. Like the carriageway, the house was in dire need of attention, and if Evan was any judge of the matter, the place would need at least five thousand spent on it to bring it to something resembling livability.

Presumably, the ebony double doors of the entrance were the originals, for time and weather had warped them, leaving gaps at the frame wide enough to admit even the mildest of winter winds and possibly a bit of snow. As well, the roof was in need of rethatching, and if the precarious leaning of the front chimneys was anything to go by, there would not be a fireplace in the entire house that did not smoke.

Not that it mattered. Evan hoped to be gone from the premises before a warming fire became necessary. There was no getting around it; he would be obliged to buy his way out of the mess he had made by his absurd handling of the proposal, and he was prepared to contribute as much as ten thousand pounds toward the refurbishing of the house and grounds if it would buy his escape from the Swann family for good.

A smallish groom, followed by a pack of six or eight assorted barking dogs came running from the stables to assist with the carriage horses, and while

Evan's manservant removed their boxes from the
boot, Evan raised the swan's head knocker at the
door. Within a matter of minutes, the left door was
opened, though not without a good deal of squeaking and creaking, and Evan was greeted by an aged
butler wearing a moth-eaten wig and faded livery.

"Lord Trent," the ancient said, taking Evan's
card, then inclining his head in what passed for a
bow. "Please come in. Sir Beecham is expecting
you."

I will wager he is! If the threadbare carpet and the
peeling paint in the vestibule were anything to go
by, the interior of the house was in no better shape
than the exterior, and Evan saw the ten thousand
pounds creep closer to fifteen thousand.

Though he felt like a chicken being led to his
own plucking, Evan followed the servant, who ushered him down a short corridor and invited him to
be seated in what must have been the morning
room. It was a pleasant enough apartment, with
lemon-yellow wallpaper and faded yellow brocade on
the settee and companion chairs, and had there
been at least one surface that was not being used to
hold an assortment of colored papers, watercolor
paints, grosgrain ribbons, feathers, scissors, and
paste, he might have taken a seat and been quite
comfortable.

Since all the chairs were in use, Evan walked over
to a pair of French windows and gazed out past a
set of stone steps that led to a rather pretty little
knot garden. He had stood there for several minutes
when he heard the door open. Almost immediately,
someone gasped.

"Your pardon," said a feminine voice, "but I had no idea anyone was h—"

She got no farther, for Evan had turned around, causing the vixen to choke on her final word.

And vixen she was, literally, for three quarters of her face was covered by a mask that was a perfect replica of a fox's muzzle, pointed snout and all. In addition, she had fitted a pair of furry peaked ears over her own ears and had pulled her coppery red hair to the back of her head, fashioning it into something resembling a fox's bushy tail.

Red hair! It wanted only that!

No one had to tell Evan that this tall, rather thin female was Miss Lydia Swann; he knew it instinctively. She could be no one else, not the way his luck was going. Attired in a loose-fitting, plain brown frock that was covered by an apron liberally spattered by watercolor paints, she was the very antithesis of the neat, curvaceous twins he had met in Bath.

"Lord Trent?"

Trying for a calm he did not feel, Evan bowed. "At your service, madam."

"Blast," she said inelegantly. "Sir, you are unconscionably late!"

"Late?"

"Yes, and as a result, we have already wasted a full day."

Two

Understandably taken aback by this unorthodox beginning, Evan merely stared at the female in the fox mask. Had she gone mad, or had he?

As if in answer to his unasked question, she said, "Your pardon, sir. You must think me deranged. I assure you, I am not. It is just—" She got no further, for she began to laugh, a situation that made Evan long to walk over and give her fox's tail a good yank.

Lydia had not wanted to laugh, of course. Unfortunately, the choice was either laugh or give in to the nervousness that filled her upon first seeing the gentleman with the angry eyes. And angry they were, though she could not imagine why they should be so; after all, there was no way Lord Trent could know of her father's scheme. Or of her own plan.

In any event, when Lydia had walked into the morning room, thinking it as empty as when she had left it, she had been unprepared for the jolt to her senses caused by the unexpected sight of the tall, well-built gentleman in the beautifully tailored dove-gray coat. At first she had gasped; then she had tried to apologize for her gaucherie. Then, of course, she had completely lost her train of thought, for the man had turned, directing the full force of his dark brown eyes upon her. Something in those eyes had made her want to step back a bit, put some distance between them.

She was not frightened, of course, just momentarily taken by surprise by the strength that emanated from the man. Lydia was accustomed to her blustering father, who ranted like a petulant child whenever he felt his wishes were not being given the attention they deserved. It was immediately obvious that the man before her was of a different sort entirely. Somehow, Lydia knew without question that Lord Trent would never rant. Never rave. Never even raise his voice. There would be no need.

According to her father, Evan Trent had once been a member of the Royal Navy, a battle-hardened officer who had been decorated for bravery. It stood to reason that such a man—one who had led other men into battle, one who had distinguished himself under fire—would possess a strong personality. It was this strength that Lydia felt all the way across the room, and it caused her knees to tremble, a nervousness that was totally unlike her. So, she had laughed.

"Forgive me for my ill-timed humor, sir. You cannot know it, but my life seems to be following a pattern of late, one involving poor timing and unexpected meetings."

"Of course."

The coolness of Evan's reply caused the smile to disappear from the young woman's lips, the only part of her face he could actually see. She rallied immediately, however, and after squaring her shoulders, she crossed the room, coming toward him with her hand outstretched politely. "I am Miss Swann. Miss *Lydia* Swann."

Evan schooled his face to show no reaction to the name. "Ma'am," he said politely. He would have taken her hand, but at the last instant she glanced down, apparently realized her fingers were smeared with paint and paste, and snatched her hand away.

"Be seated, if you please, my lord, while I see if Gordon has ordered refreshments."

When he made no move toward the furniture, Miss Swann looked about her, muttered something beneath her breath, then hurried to empty one of the slipper chairs of what Evan now recognized to be a dozen or so masks, most of them cunningly wrought animal faces.

"For the children in my Sunday-school class," she said, as if that explained the disarray. "There are twenty boys and girls in all, and I promised that if everyone could read the first primer by harvest time, I would host an All Hallow's Eve party to end all parties. I am pleased to say the children have kept their end of the bargain. Now, as you can see, I am in the process of keeping mine."

After clearing a chair for Evan, she did not seek the butler as she had said, but pushed aside a stack of colored paper on the settee and disposed herself upon the edge of the faded yellow brocade. "Speaking of bargains, my lord, I am persuaded there is one you and I should strike. Now, while my father is away from the house."

Evan stiffened. Here was plain speaking indeed. "I cannot think what you mean, madam."

She sighed, as if put out of countenance by his apparent obtuseness. "Believe me, sir. It would be better for us both if we took advantage of these moments alone, for there is a matter of business that you and I should get settled."

He could not believe this woman. Did she think to force him into making her a declaration? "Actually, ma'am, I believe what I have to say is best left until your father returns."

"Trust me, my lord, it is not. Not if you wish to leave Swannleigh Manor as unencumbered as when you arrived."

Thinking it wisest to remain silent, Evan said nothing.

"I know," she continued, "that what I am about to say will take you by surprise, but I must apprise you of the totally foolish notion my father has taken into his head."

"I am listening, madam."

Though the young lady placed her hands demurely in her lap, the dignified effect was spoiled by the fox mask she seemed to have forgotten she wore. "First, allow me to tell you, sir, that I have read your letter."

"My letter," Evan repeated, stalling for time.

"As a matter of fact, I read it through several times, and though the wording of your proposal was ambiguous at best, *I* realize, as does my father, that it was your intention to offer for Clarissanne."

Clarissanne. So, that was the older twin's name.

"Unfortunately, sir, I must inform you that Clarissanne is spoken for. As is Clorinda. Both my sisters returned from Bath engaged to be married."

Oddly enough, Evan was relieved to hear it. "I cannot say I am surprised, ma'am. The young ladies were quite popular. Be so good as to convey my best wishes to both the Miss Swanns."

"I shall, sir, and thank you." She hesitated a moment. "Since I have no way of judging the degree of your attachment to my sister, pray allow me to offer my sincerest hope that this news does not pain you too much."

"Er, no, ma'am. Not too much."

She cleared her throat, her embarrassment obvious. "However," she continued, "that is not an end to the matter."

Here it comes! To let her know that he was not some pawn to be used in her and her father's matrimonial game, he replied rather coldly, "You must excuse my obvious dull-wittedness, ma'am, but I should think a prior engagement would nullify my offer."

"Normally it would, had you asked specifically for Clarissanne. Regrettably, you did not."

While Evan remained perfectly still, waiting for her to confirm his worst fears, the speaker took a deep breath, as if to fortify herself. "Because you asked for my father's eldest daughter, he hopes to convince you that you are now officially engaged to me. Which I assure you, my lord, you are not."

Surprise mingled with relief as Evan stared at the young woman across from him. Her paint-stained fingers were laced together so tightly he suspected the circulation must be seriously curtailed, and her lips trembled slightly, betraying the discomfort she obviously felt at having to reveal such a humiliating and ignoble plot.

Her embarrassment further relieved Evan's mind, giving him hope that all was not lost. "Excuse me," he said, "but would you do something for me?"

"Of course, sir. What is it?"

"Would you remove your mask?"

Her hands flew to her head, convincing Evan that she had, indeed, forgotten the disguise.

"Though the vixen's face is most cunningly wrought, ma'am, I feel at a decided disadvantage discussing such a life-altering matter as a betrothal with someone who is wearing furry ears and a pointed snout."

"Your pardon, Lord Trent. I had forgotten I wore the mask."

Evan watched her remove the furry ears, then untie the grosgrain ribbons that held the fox face in place. When she placed the mask beside her on the settee, then looked up at him, what he saw took him quite by surprise. Hers was not the angelic beauty of her twin sisters, but Miss Lydia Swann was by no means an ugly duckling.

Except for the light sprinkling of freckles across her nose, hers was a flawless complexion, and her fern-green eyes were framed by surprisingly dark lashes. Furthermore, there was an upward tilt at the corners of her mouth that hinted at a happy disposition. Were it not for the unfortunate red hair, she would be a rather pretty girl. Not pretty enough to suit his taste, of course, but definitely a handsome female.

"Now," he said, "let me see if I have this correctly. Your father wishes to convince me that I am betrothed to you. You, however, do not wish to fall in with his plans."

"No, my lord, I do not."

Though more than happy to hear that she had no designs on him, some imp inside Evan would not let him leave well enough alone. "If I may ask, ma'am, have you something against the married state?"

"Nothing at all. In fact, I should very much like to be married."

"Just not to me."

"Not to any man, my lord, who does not love me to distraction."

At the look of disgust on Lord Trent's face, Lydia felt warmth invade her cheeks. She had not meant to give voice to such a blatantly romantic notion, but the sentiment was honest, and she made no apologies for it. She positively longed for romance.

All her life Lydia had dreamed of being madly, passionately in love. She craved the excitement, the intoxicating feeling of being swept off her feet by a daring, charismatic man who could not live without her—a man whose every thought mirrored her thoughts, whose every goal matched her own. A man who was the missing half of her soul, and whose missing half she would prove to be.

A man like Sebastian Osborne.

Fearing she might become lost in her usual dreams of Sebastian, whose very name was music to her heart, Lydia forced her attention back to the present. Since the day before yesterday, when her father had shown her Lord Trent's letter, Lydia had thought of nothing but Sir Beecham's foolish scheme, and she had come up with a scheme of her own. To succeed, though, it needed Lord Trent's cooperation.

When she looked at the gentleman, however, looked into his square-jawed, rather uncompromising face and his dark, unreadable eyes, she felt some reservations about his agreeing to a plan that involved subterfuge.

"I wonder, sir, do you know my father?"

Lord Trent shook his head.

"He is an uncomplicated man," she said, "interested in sport and little else. But like many uncomplicated people, once he gets an idea into his head, he clings to it with the tenacity of a bulldog with a fresh bone between its teeth."

"And?" the visitor said. "Your point is?"

"My point, sir, is that Papa has gotten it into his head that you and I are as good as betrothed, and he believes that as a gentleman, you will feel it is your duty to honor your proposal."

"And?" he said again, his square jaw appearing even more stubborn than before.

"And," she replied, "to give Papa time to lose interest in this betrothal, time to let go his hold on this particular *bone,* I suggest that you and I go along with the plan. But only for the next two weeks."

The viscount's brown eyes had become cold as ice. "Do you take me for a fool, madam? Pretending to be engaged is not the answer."

"It is *my* answer, my lord. Unless, of course, you would prefer the real engagement my father has in mind?"

The gentleman's haughty expression relaxed slightly. "Surely you must see, madam, that such a pretense would only sink me—us—farther into that inescapable trap."

"You cannot have been paying attention, sir. I said we should pretend to be engaged for only two weeks. During that time, the first of my two objectives will be to prove to one and all that you and I do not suit. At the end of the fortnight, no matter what has or has not happened in my life, you have my word that I will call off the betrothal and return to my home in time for the All Hallow's Eve party."

"Return to your home? I must have missed something. Where will you be until that time?"

"Why, at your home, sir, being presented to your mother."

He muttered something Lydia did not hear; then he said, "You mentioned two objectives, Miss Swann. What, if I may ask, is your second?"

"While at Trent Park, my lord, I wish to travel to Osborne Grange, which, if my calculations are correct, is roughly ten miles from your home."

"Osborne Grange? Do you mean Squire Osborne's place?"

"Yes. Are you acquainted with the squire?"

"Slightly." Recalling that the ruddy-faced, portly squire was justice of the peace for the neighborhood of Alderbury, Evan said, "Forgive me, Miss Swann, but have you business at the Grange?"

"In a manner of speaking. The squire is married to a lady who was once my mother's sister-in-law, and I have in mind to visit with my aunt and my two cousins."

To Evan's surprise, Lydia Swann's face turned quite pink. "Actually," she said, "I . . ."

"You?" he prompted.

She took a deep breath, then let the crux of her plan more or less fall from her lips. "In all truth, my lord, though I shall be happy to see Aunt Minerva and my cousins, my primary wish is to renew my acquaintance with my aunt's stepson."

"That would be Squire Osborne's son?"

"Yes. Do you know Sebastian?"

"I do not believe so. Is he much like his father?"

"Not at all. Not in the least!" she added, apparently aghast at the suggestion that the young man might resemble the stout, though good-natured squire. Then, with a sigh, she added, "Sebastian Osborne is the handsomest, the most daring, the most romantic man in the entire world, and within the next two weeks, I intend to do all within my power to inspire him to want to marry me."

Three

"Since you never came right out and made me a formal offer of marriage," she said, in answer to Evan's question as to how she convinced Sir Beecham to let her travel to Alderbury, "I promised Papa that while I visited with Lady Trent, I would employ every device at my disposal to ensure that I came home with a betrothal ring on my finger."

While she stared out the window of the traveling coach, pretending an interest in one of the numerous half-timbered Tudor homes that dotted the rolling green landscape, an imp of a smile lifted the corners of her mouth. "Of course," she added, "I may have failed to mention the name of the gentleman whose affection I hoped to secure along with the ring."

Evan chuckled. "Madam, considering your knack for duplicity, I am beginning to think I was most fortunate to have escaped . . . er, what I mean is—"

"I know just what you mean, my lord, and I am in complete agreement with your assessment. I am too duplicitous for you, and you are too . . ." She paused, as if searching for the proper word, and in the next instant her cheeks turned a bright red.

"Too?" Evan prompted.

"I should not have spoken, my lord."

"Oh, no, madam. You do not get out of it that easily. You were on the verge of saying that I was too *something* for you. I should like to know what that is. Too rough-hewn, perhaps?"

Taking her silence for assent, he continued. "I was seven years in the Royal Navy, and I spent months at a time at sea, the majority of my companions a set of crude, unsophisticated sailors. After years of such company, I fear my manners could use a bit of polishing. And, of course, I need not mention the toll the sun and salty air take on a seafaring man's face. As a result of my time at sea, I possess neither the pretty words nor the handsome countenance needed to appeal to a romantic young lady like yourself."

"I must disagree," she said. "Especially regarding the subject of your manners. Compared to my father's usual brusque behavior, your conduct is . . ."

"Yes?"

She shook her head. "For the sake of family loyalty, perhaps I should say no more on that particular subject. And since I seem to be walking into all manner of verbal traps, I believe it would be safest if I forget all topics save one—the matter of your looks."

Evan had not meant to introduce himself as a topic for discussion, but his traveling companion continued as though she had been invited to give her opinion.

"If the truth be told, my lord, I think you a very handsome man."

Taken quite by surprise, Evan was about to thank her for the compliment when she added, "You are not nearly as handsome as Sebastian, of course, but that has more to do with the uncompromising angles of your face than with your tanned skin."

"Miss Swann giveth, and Miss Swann taketh away."

"Not at all, sir. Why, with your thick brown hair and your dark brown eyes, you want only a patch over your left eye to put me in mind of Lord Timothy Tambour. And I am persuaded there must be literally thousands of young ladies who fancy themselves in love with Lord Tambour."

"With whom?"

"The privateer in Mrs. Esther Widmore's latest novel, *Lady Jane's Buccaneer.* Tambour is both handsome and daring, and when he whisked Lady Jane Vickers away from the evil Sir Damian DeValle, my heart very nearly leaped from my—"

Evan groaned. "Never tell me, madam, that you read novels."

"But I do read them, anytime I can put my hands on one. And why should I not? I *like* novels, and I see no reason why I should apologize for reading them."

"I never said you should—"

"If you mean to tell me, my lord, that there is some greater virtue in what you men enjoy—chasing a poor defenseless fox across a field, or watching two cocks peck out each other's eyes, or sitting up until all hours of the morning consuming bottles of brandy until you become disgustingly inebriated, then risking your fortune on the turn of a card—do not bother. Novels are an innocent and enjoyable pastime, and though a bit pricey at the time of purchase, they can be read again and again at no further expenditure. As well, no actual blood is ever spilled, and to my knowledge, no one has ever lost their home or their fortune at the turn of a book page."

Evan merely stared at the young woman who sat on the front-facing seat of the coach. Lydia Swann was nothing if not outspoken, and Evan was beginning to learn that if he did not wish to hear an answer, he had better not ask the question.

When he had asked her yesterday, not half an hour after meeting her, how she had come to hatch this scheme to ensnare her aunt's stepson, she had replied quite honestly, "I do not wish to *entrap* Sebastian. I merely wish to give him the opportunity, now that I am all grown-up, to fall in love with me, as I fell in love with him eight years ago. I was but sixteen when he and I met, and at that time my figure had not yet devel—Er, what I mean to say is, I was still very thin."

From what Evan could see, Lydia Swann was still rather thin, although she looked quite nice today, with her hair arranged neatly beneath a chip-straw bonnet whose umber-colored ribbons perfectly matched her pelisse. The autumn shade suited her complexion and brought out a trace of gold in her green eyes, and when she smiled, as she had done often during the past four hours of their trip, Evan was forced to admit there was a certain *appealing* quality about her.

Though he could understand her desire to have this Osborne fellow see her now that she was all grown-up, especially since she had been in love with him for a third of her life, Evan had but one caveat: what if those years had not been as kind to Sebastian Osborne as they had been to Lydia Swann? The fellow might no longer be the handsome Greek god she remembered. He might be given to drink, or gluttony, either of which would have altered his appearance, and not for the better.

"Something occurs to me," Evan said. "What if your would-be fiancé is no longer at the Grange? Many gentlemen his age prefer to reside in town."

The sudden change of subject did not bother his companion in the least. "He does keep rooms in town. However, his father's fiftieth birthday is the twenty-fifth of this month, and his family has made plans to mark the occasion with a fancy dress party.

"And," she continued, "I have it on good authority that Sebastian has promised to spend the entire month of October at home with the family. Even so, the days are passing quickly, and I have only what remains of the month to make Sebastian fall in love with me. That is why I was upset that you did not arrive at Swannleigh earlier."

"Had you the full month," Evan said, "it would do you no good if the gentleman should prove to be betrothed to another. You have not seen him in years, it could be that he—"

"Sebastian is not betrothed."

As if she read Evan's next thought, she added, "And before you suggest that he might be in love with someone else, let me assure you that he remains as heartfree as he is handsome. Of course, the squire would like to see his only son form an attachment to some well-connected lady with a dowry of fifteen or twenty thousand, but I assure you, Sebastian has no such ambition."

Since Lydia had not mentioned that her swain was bookish, or army mad, or had dreams of a religious or political future, Evan was about to ask her if the gentleman had *any* ambition at all, other than cutting a figure as a dashing blade, when the coachman slowed the horses. The team responded, and in a matter of seconds the coachman turned them to the left and urged them through the square, gritstone posts that gave access to the crushed-stone carriageway of Trent Park.

"We have arrived," he said. "Welcome, Miss Swann, to my home."

At his words, his companion sat forward where she could see out the window, her eyes alight with interest.

The carriageway stretched due north for about a quarter of a mile through a rolling, wooded parkland, with hills in the background dotted by white sheep; then it took a forty-five-degree turn westward. Only when the coach was on the second half of the approach was the house visible. Like the entrance posts, the Tudor residence was fashioned of the local grayish brown gritstone, and also like the posts, it stood square and tall and invincible. Consisting of thirty or more rooms, the main structure was four stories, while the east and west wings were three stories each.

Evan loved his home. He always had, and for him, to see the place after a time away from it was to love it anew. Upon each return, he looked at the large, sixteenth-century edifice with a pleasure that was undiminished by repetition.

Though he had never cared what anyone else thought of his home, he returned his attention to Lydia Swann, unexpectedly eager to see her reaction. "Do you like it?" he asked.

"Like it? I should be hard to please if I did not.

The prospect alone is beautiful enough to inspire one to poetry. As for the house, words fail me."

She said no more for a time; then, when Evan saw her lips twitch with the effort to hide her smile, he could not refrain from asking her what was in her thoughts.

"Nothing of any *real* consequence, my lord. Except that after seeing your magnificent estate, I have revised my estimate of your manners and your looks. Both of which, you must know, have improved immeasurably in the past two minutes."

The statement was so outrageous that Evan laughed aloud.

"It wants only for you to tell me," she continued, "that one may go boating on that stretch of river I see at the end of those beautifully landscaped terraces, and I shall be casting poor Sebastian aside and setting my cap for you."

Evan held his breath for only a split second; then he heard her soft laughter. "Minx!" he said.

He was beginning to like this red-haired duckling. If the truth be known, he preferred her to either of her beautiful swanlike sisters. But the fact remained that even after seeing the lovely twins again, he still had no desire to marry one of them, or anyone else, for that matter. In fact, he felt so relieved to be coming home still unbetrothed, that he had decided to postpone any farther wife hunting until after Lydia's two-week visit was accomplished and he had returned her to her family.

The coachman reined in the horses, and immediately two footmen and a butler hurried down the three steps to assist the viscount and his guest to alight. "Ah, Palmer," Evan said, acknowledging the middle-aged butler's rather formal bow. "As you see, I have brought Miss Swann for a visit with my mother. Is she here?"

The butler inclined his head. "Lady Trent is in the burgundy morning room, my lord."

"Very good. Please see that an apartment is made ready for our guest, and choose one of the maids to attend her. Meanwhile, we should like some refreshments." Evan looked to Lydia. "Tea and sandwiches?" he asked.

At her almost imperceptible nod, the butler bowed again. "As you wish, my lord."

Leaving the servants to handle the details, Evan took Lydia by the arm and led her down a long corridor toward the morning room the family used in the cooler months, a room that was at the rear of the east wing. To his surprise, the loquacious young woman was unusually quiet, and when he glanced down at her, he noticed that her cheeks appeared rather pale. "What is amiss? Are you ill?"

"Not ill," she replied softly. "Petrified. Now that the time has come to meet Lady Trent, I begin to suspect that this entire mock-betrothal scheme is foolish beyond permission."

"Madam," he said, "it always was."

At his reply, she gave him a look that said she would choke before she would cry craven.

"As you wish," he said, pausing at the closed door. "Before you meet my mother, however, let me hear you call me by my name. If we are to pull this off, I think it only fitting that we be on a first-name basis."

When she said nothing, he said, "Lydia? Do you know my name?"

"Of course I know it," she snapped. "I am nervous, not deranged. Your name is Evan."

"Good girl." He said no more, merely opened the door and ushered her inside. "Mother," he began. "I have a surprise for you."

"My dear boy," Lady Trent said. "Come in, for I have a surprise for you as well. Look who has come to pay us a nice long visit."

While Lydia stared across the cozy room, which was decorated in shades of burgundy and silver-gray, a short, but noticeably muscular gentleman wearing the blue uniform of the Royal Navy rose from the wing chair opposite Lady Trent's. Walking with the unmistakable rolling gate of a sailor, he came forward, his tanned face softened by a wide smile and his callused hand extended to Evan. "Surprised to see me, old boy?"

"Michael! You old sea dog. What are you doing in Cheshire?"

"The ship is at anchor in the harbor at Liverpool, currently out of discipline. So I thought I would give myself the pleasure of calling upon your lady mother. You, of course, I could see or not see, and it would be of no consequence."

The naval gentleman gave the lie to his words by catching Lord Trent in a bear hug and lifting the much taller man completely off the ground. Evan took the greeting in good part, but after a moment or two he broke his friend's hold by threatening to run him through if he did not unhand him immediately. "Besides," he added, "though you have the manners of a Barbary ape, I cannot leave Miss Swann standing about forever. Therefore, if you will be so good as to move aside, I should like to introduce the young lady to my mother."

"Miss Swann?" Lady Trent said, rising from her chair. "My dear child, forgive me for not greeting you, but I did not expect—"

The words, like her ladyship's welcoming smile, ended abruptly. "But, Evan, this is not—" Once again she halted, only this time, generations of good breeding came to her rescue. "Miss Swann," she said, coming forward, her hand extended in greeting, "what a pleasure to meet you."

"You are very kind, ma'am." Lydia curtsied; then she took the proffered hand, though she did not look overlong into those probing, dark brown eyes— eyes that gazed first at Lydia, then at Evan. "I hope my unexpected arrival is not inconvenient."

Lady Trent assured her it was not. "I am always happy to welcome any of my son's friends. Did I not meet your mother and two of your sisters this past spring, while at Bath?"

"Yes, ma'am. I believe you did."

"But you did not accompany them?"

"No, ma'am. I had planned to make the trip, but due to a most unfortunate accident, I was obliged to remain at home."

"An accident? How disappointing for you. I trust you were not seriously injured."

"Only my pride, ma'am."

While her ladyship waited quietly, apparently hoping for enlightenment as to what had brought a complete stranger to her home, Lydia looked down at the handsome silver and blue Axminster carpet on the floor, wishing she was anywhere but at Trent Park. Knowing herself for an unmitigated fraud, if she had been in possession of a magic wand, she would have waved it at that moment and whisked herself back to Lower Dewes.

"I . . ." Lydia's tongue felt as though it were stuck to the roof of her mouth, and she had trouble giving voice to the well-rehearsed story of the engagement. It was one thing to concoct a Banbury tale to hood-wink her father into allowing her to travel to Trent Park; it was quite another thing to look this very nice lady in the face and utter that same falsehood. "I was unable to travel last spring," she said at last, "so . . . er, so Evan was kind enough to bring me here for a fortnight. I have relatives close by, and I . . . that is, he . . ."

"I thought," Evan said, coming to her rescue, "that Miss Swann would be more comfortable if she visited her relatives on a daily basis, while remaining here at the Park."

As a logical explanation, it lacked merit, but after Lady Trent gave her son a searching look, she apparently chose to accept the convoluted story. "If you will," she said to Evan, "ring the bell for Palmer. I am persuaded Miss Swann must be famished after her journey. As for me, I could use a cup of tea. Perhaps a very strong cup."

"Sheer lunacy," Lady Trent said later, when she and her son were alone in the sitting room adjoining her bedchamber. "Not that I blame the young lady for taking what must appear her one chance to secure the gentleman's regard, but if her fumbling explanation to me is any indication, it would appear Miss Swann is not very good at dissembling. I wonder how she expected to carry off such a tarradiddle. And I wonder, as well, what made her change her story."

Evan shrugged his broad shoulders. "Who can say. I suspect it was easier to fabricate an engagement in theory than in actuality. As you will discover, Lydia is a very forthright young lady, often disconcertingly honest."

"Honesty *can* be a disconcerting quality," his mother agreed, "but I suspect that is only because one meets with it so seldom. In any case, the fewer people who hear of this spurious engagement the better. And since Miss Swann was so good as to refuse to go along with her father's plan to hold you to that idiotic proposal, I suppose the least we can do is to go along with her only slightly less idiotic plan to capture Squire Osborne's son."

After a few moments of silence, she asked, "What sort of fellow is he? Do you know him?"

Evan shook his head. "All I know is that Lydia fancies herself in love with him. According to her, the gentleman is unbelievably handsome, and possessed of all the virtues—vigor, courage, daring—the kind of fellow every young girl dreams of. And the sort they never forget. Even after eight years."

"Eight years! What foolishness is this? Does the girl live on a desert island, that she has met no other personable young men in all that time?"

"As to that, ma'am, I cannot say. I know Sir Beecham could not afford to give her a London season. But even if she had gone to town, that is no guarantee that another man could have replaced Sebastian in Lydia's affections."

His mother made a sound of disgust. "That is

pure fustian, my boy. Put a healthy young female in contact with someone of the opposite sex, give the pair time to get to know one another, and I promise you, the young woman will soon forget an eight-year infatuation."

"Ah, but you should know, ma'am, that Lydia Swann is a very romantic young lady. In fact, she informs me that I put her in mind of some pirate or other. *Sans* the eye patch, of course."

"A pirate?"

"Yes, a Lord Tambourine, or some such."

"Lord Timothy Tambour? From Mrs. Widmore's latest novel?"

"Why, yes. I believe that was the name."

Having read *Lady Jane's Buccaneer* just a few days earlier, Lady Trent was quite familiar with the very dashing, very handsome gentleman-privateer. So Evan reminded the romantic Miss Lydia of Lord Timothy Tambour, did he? How interesting.

Mary Trent smiled, and though she wondered if their guest reminded Evan of anyone, her ladyship was not so foolish as to ask the question. A wise mother knew better than to pry into her son's affairs—most especially if those affairs looked promising.

Feeling that she was entitled to some tiny crumb of information, however, just enough to assuage her curiosity, she said, "Too bad Miss Lydia has not the beauty of her sisters. The twins are truly diamonds of the first water." When Evan did not rise to the bait, Lady Trent tried another approach. "And yet, Miss Lydia has a pleasing way about her, would you not agree?"

"Quite pleasing," Evan said. "Unfortunately, there is still the matter of the red hair."

There was never any accounting for taste, of course, and scarcely two hours later Evan discovered that his closest friend, Captain Michael Danforth, had no aversion whatever to red hair. To the contrary, he apparently found it quite charming, for when Evan entered the formal blue drawing room, where the family gathered prior to the evening meal, the naval gentleman appeared all but enthralled by the lady with the bright-colored hair.

Lydia stood in the embrasure of one of the floor-to-ceiling windows that overlooked the rose garden at the rear of the house, and Captain Danforth stood beside her, laughing uproariously at something the lady had just said to him.

"Miss Swann," he said between bouts of laughter, "if you will forgive my saying so, you are what my grandfather calls a caution."

Lydia chuckled, though Evan did not think what his friend had said was particularly amusing. "A caution, am I? Since you saw fit to ask my pardon for saying it, Captain, could it be that 'caution' is some cant phrase meaning I am a hoyden?"

"Not at all, ma'am. Perhaps I should have said that you are an original."

Caution? Original? What the deuce was Michael thinking of? Why, if it were anyone but his oldest friend, Evan would have thought the fellow was making up to Lydia.

Since the pair at the window was too engrossed in their conversation to notice that Evan had entered the room, he went directly to the console table and poured himself a glass of sherry. Then, while he sipped at the nutty-flavored wine, he returned his attention to Lydia and Michael.

The two of them were much of the same height, and as a consequence, Lydia, who was rather tall for a female, did not need to look up to the captain. If the animation of her face was anything to go by, however, she did not mind looking directly into his eyes, for what Michael lacked in stature, he more than made up for in brawn and masculine charm. Gray-eyed, with short light brown hair, he had never numbered among the Adonises, and yet the ladies— be they sixteen or sixty—all seemed to like him.

As for the captain, judging by his smiles, the tall young lady suited him just fine. In truth, when Evan looked Lydia over from her pert little nose to her slippered feet, he could find nothing to dislike in her. True, her bosom was small, but her exposed shoulders appeared surprisingly soft and feminine, the skin smooth and creamy looking, and the gentle draping of her gold sarcenet dinner dress could not hide the indisputable curves of the delicate figure beneath.

"What did I do?" Evan heard her say, obviously repeating a question asked her by the captain. "What *could* I do?"

At the sound of her amused voice, Evan swallowed his sherry in one gulp. Unaccountably irritated, he gave up all pretense that he was not eavesdropping on his guests' conversation. "Under the circumstances," Lydia continued, "I did what any sensible person would have done. I ran. Unfortunately, Captain, I was not fast enough."

"Never say so," Michael said. "Did he get you?"

In lieu of an answer, the young lady placed her thumb and forefinger on either side of her nose and pinched the nostrils shut.

"By Jove!" Michael said, trying not to laugh. "You must have smelled awful."

"I assure you, Captain, 'awful' does not begin to describe it."

For a moment, all was quiet; then Michael burst out laughing. At the sound, Evan slammed his glass down on the console, nearly shattering the crystal; then he strode purposefully down the long room to the window embrasure. "If I may ask," he said, staring rather belligerently at his oldest friend, "what the devil is so amusing?"

Captain Danforth was spared having to answer his host, for Lady Trent chose that moment to enter the room. "Forgive me," she said, "if I have kept you waiting." Then, to her son she said, "I was with Jack, doing my best to persuade him to join us later for tea, so he might pay his respects to Captain Danforth and make Miss Swann's acquaintance."

"And did you succeed?" Evan asked. "Did he agree to come down?"

"He agreed, and yet I cannot be certain that he will not renege at the last moment. We shall just have to wait and see. And hope for the best."

Four

Dinner was a lively affair, with Captain Danforth keeping them all entertained with tales of the exotic places to which he had sailed in the five years since Evan had been wounded at Trafalgar and had given up his commission in the Royal Navy.

Lydia had wondered how Evan had gotten the slight scar that bisected his left eyebrow. It was not a disfiguring reminder by any means; if anything, it made him appear rather mysterious, like a man with a past. "You were with Admiral Nelson?" she asked.

Evan nodded. "Michael and I both were, and no finer man ever lived than Admiral Horatio Nelson."

"Here, here!" Captain Danforth said, raising his glass in toast to the fallen hero, the man whose victory had broken Napoleon's navy and made Great Britain the ruler of the seas.

A silence followed the toast, and into that silence Lydia asked a question that had been on her mind since she and Evan had arrived that afternoon. "Captain Danforth," she said, "may I ask you a question?"

"Of course, Miss Lydia. Ask, and I shall do all within my power to supply the answer."

"This afternoon, sir, you mentioned that your ship was at anchor in the harbor at Liverpool, currently out of discipline. I am unfamiliar with that term, and I wondered if you would be so good as to explain the significance of—"

"Mother!" Evan said, interrupting Lydia midsentence. "Do you suppose Jack is waiting for us in the drawing room?"

"Yes," Lady Trent said, her face decidedly pink beneath the light dusting of powder. "I wondered about that myself."

Though a footman had just brought in a silver serving tray upon which reposed a Chantilly cake flanked by dishes of *puits d'amour,* her ladyship laid her napkin beside her plate and rose from the table, signifying that the meal was at an end. "Come, Miss Swann. We will leave the gentlemen to their port."

Lydia, aware that she had unknowingly committed a faux pas, followed her hostess's example and laid her napkin aside. It was obvious she had asked something she should not have, but she had no idea what that might be. After rising from the table, she took one last look at Evan and the captain, who stood politely, and though the gentlemen's swarthy complexions could never be said to show embarrassment, Lydia was certain both men were disconcerted. Feeling her own cheeks grow warm, she said no more, merely joined her hostess and quietly exited the dining room.

As soon as she and Lady Trent were back in the blue drawing room, Lydia said, "Your pardon, ma'am, if I said something I should not have, but—"

Her ladyship put her finger across her lips to indicate her wish for silence; then she looked all around the room, to make certain her nephew was not sitting quietly in some corner. Jack might have lost his ability to hear, but his aunt did not wish to speak in front of him without at least trying to include him in the conversation.

Finding the room empty, save for herself and her guest, she reached over and patted Lydia's hand. "Do not give it another thought, my dear. An innocent young lady could not be expected to know about such things as ships out of discipline."

"Which is exactly why I made such an error! Because I did not know. Really, ma'am, it is too vexatious for words, this pretense we females are expected to enact when anything of a remotely earthy nature is seen or mentioned."

Not yet finished, she added, "And even when we know full well what is happening, we are expected to feign ignorance. Why, only let some gentleman drive by a group of ladies while his mistress is seated beside him in his curricle—a gentleman even the most punctilious of hostesses would welcome into her home that very evening—and all the ladies within sight of the curricle will pretend they do not see the pair. Anyone watching the ladies with their blank faces could be forgiven for thinking them as mindless as sheep."

Momentarily startled by this unexpected passion, Lady Trent stared openmouthed at her guest.

"Furthermore," Lydia continued, not yet ready to abandon her feeling of ill-use, "I wish you would tell me, ma'am, how I am to know when to join the sheep, if I am kept in the dark as to the significance of the subjects I must avoid?"

Her composure reclaimed, Lady Trent said, "Your argument has merit, Miss Swann, and since I have never been overfond of females who pretend ignorance of even the most innocent of humankind's basic instincts, I am prepared to answer the question you asked of Captain Danforth."

Crossing the room to the blue velvet settee nearest the fireplace, she bid her guest sit beside her, then waited until Lydia complied with the invitation. "I assume, my dear, that you are aware of the difficulty the Royal Navy has in maintaining crews aboard its thousand or more ships."

"Yes, ma'am. I have heard that sailors sometimes desert their ships, leaving the crew shorthanded. And when one considers the hardships an ordinary seaman must endure—months at sea, long, toiling hours, then being expected to consume weevil-infested food and scummy drinking water—it is not difficult to understand why he would wish to try another lifestyle. Especially," she added, "if the seaman was 'pressed' into service in the first place."

"So, you know about the press gangs?"

"I do, ma'am, and I ask myself how a civilized nation can condone such a deplorable practice. Gangs of men paid to roam the backstreets of the port towns, knocking unwary men in the head and delivering them to ships where they are 'pressed' into His Majesty's service. I cannot say it speaks well for our navy or for our government. Or for the other countries that countenance impressment."

Choosing to leave a debate over ethics and politics for another time, Lady Trent said, "If a captain has a full crew, he has no need of press gangs."

"Yes, but—"

"Therefore, you will understand why a wise ship's captain will anchor his ship out in the harbor, at a distance too far from shore to allow his men to jump overboard and swim for land."

"But that, too, is heartless, and—"

"In the mean time," she added before Lydia could give voice to further objections, "the captains know that their crews need . . . shall we say, *diversion*. So to give them an opportunity for uninhibited activity, all the officers leave the ship, thus rendering it 'out of discipline.'

"Of course," she continued, taking care not to look directly at her unmarried guest, "while the officers are away, the boatswain, or some other trusted sailor, will be allowed the use of one of the ship's small boats to row ashore, his purpose to fetch any of the seamen's wives who are wishful of visiting their husbands aboard ship."

"Oh," Lydia said, "I think I understand you, ma'am. What you are *not* saying is that most of the females brought back to the ship are merely wives for an evening. And, of course, that is why Evan and Captain Danforth found the subject embarrassing and were so eager to have me out of the room."

"You are very quick, Miss Swann. And, I am relieved to discover, not of a missish nature."

"And why should I be? I perfectly understand that sailors who have been at sea for months would be wishful of female companionship."

A bit surprised, Lady Trent said, "You do?"

"Of course. I am country bred, ma'am, and it would be ridiculous of me to pretend that I do not know where calves and colts come from, or why the stallions sometimes injure themselves knocking down fences to get to the mares. Or why the rooster struts among the hens, crowing about his recent activities."

After a stunned silence, Lady Trent burst out laughing. *Strutting roosters. What an apt analogy.* Her son had told her that Lydia Swann was disconcertingly honest. If the truth be told, her ladyship was much inclined to the think their red-haired guest refreshingly unaffected.

Still, when a knock sounded at the drawing-room door, the subject of sailors and ships was dropped without further comment.

"Enter," Lady Trent called.

A red-faced footmen opened the door, and after begging her ladyship's pardon, informed her that Gracie, one of the chambermaids, had fallen down the servants' stairs and appeared to have broken her ankle. "Shall I send for Doctor Reeves, my lady?"

"Oh, dear. Poor Gracie. By all means, send one of the grooms to the village for the doctor." Turning to Lydia, she said, "Pray excuse me, my dear, but I feel I must see how the girl is faring. I shall return as soon as may be."

Lady Trent had been gone less than a minute when the door opened again and a dark-haired youth entered the room, his footsteps hesitant and his boyish face set rather defensively. Almost as tall as Lydia, the lad was painfully thin—all elbows and knees—and like an overgrown puppy, his body had not yet caught up with his rather large feet and hands.

"Hello," Lydia said. She rose from the settee, and after curtsying to the lad, she met him in the middle of the room, where she offered him her hand. "How do you do?" she asked quietly.

Jack Trent bowed politely; then he shook Lydia's hand. He did not, however, return her verbal greeting.

Lydia had been informed of Jack's illness and his subsequent hearing loss, so she ignored his reticence, appreciating its cause. After making certain he was looking into her face, she asked, "Do you read lips?" the words spoken in a whisper and more slowly than was her usual speed.

The boy nodded his head. Obviously rethinking his answer, he removed a notepad and pencil from the pocket of his woolen jacket. After angrily scribbling something on the pad, he turned it toward Lydia, holding it before her face so that she was obliged to read the words.

"Yes," she said. "Lip reading is a difficult skill to master, but I am happy to know that you can do it, even if only a little. My sisters and I tried it often when we were little girls, but only Clorinda ever became really good at it."

At his questioning look, she said, "Clorinda is one of my two sisters. The three of us learned some lip reading and a bit of hand language from our uncle, a gentleman who gained those talents and more during a year spent in a Tibetan monastery, where silence was strictly enforced."

Why? Jack wrote.

"I cannot say for certain. I believe Uncle Milford wanted to sample all the world had to offer, so—"

Not him! Jack scribbled quickly. *You? Your sisters?*

"Oh. Why did the twins and I want to learn?" She chuckled, enjoying an amusing memory. "I fear our motives did not do us credit, for we found both forms of silent communication of immeasurable value in vexing our governess."

When it became obvious that Jack had missed at least half of what Lydia said, she asked for his pad and pencil. Before long, they were sitting side by side on the settee, each taking a turn at writing, with Jack asking her to show him a bit of the hand language she and her sisters had learned from their uncle.

Fully twenty minutes had passed before Evan and Captain Danforth entered the drawing room. The two gentlemen were laughing over a shared reminiscence about one of their more colorful comrades in arms, but when Evan spied Lydia and his cousin, their heads together like old friends, he stopped on the instant, his laughter gone as though it had never been. "Jack?" he said, momentarily forgetting that the lad could not hear him. "What is—"

"Evan," Lydia said, looking up from the notepad, where Jack was scribbling away. An instant later, she tapped the boy on the wrist and pointed behind him at the new arrivals.

Calling himself all kinds of fool, Evan pretended he had not spoken, and though he wanted to ask Lydia what the deuce she was doing, he suppressed his curiosity in favor of good manners. Jack and the captain shook hands, and after the boy nodded toward his cousin, he smothered a laugh behind his hand and slipped from the room, leaving both gentlemen staring after him.

"He will return," Lydia said. "He is fetching something from the schoolroom."

With that, Evan was obliged to be content. He watched Lydia rather closely while he and Michael made themselves comfortable near the fireplace, Michael in one of the lyre-back chairs, Evan standing beside the blue-tiled hearth, his elbow propped on the mantel. "So," he said, "you met my cousin."

Lydia nodded. "A nice boy. I have been telling him about my Uncle Milford Hilton who, like Captain Danforth, has led a most interesting life. Not a few years of it spent in some rather bizarre places."

"How bizarre?" the captain asked, his eyes alight with interest.

"Siam, for one," she replied. "My uncle managed a tea plantation while there. Afterward, he spent a year in a contemplative monastery located in the Himalayan Mountains. Following the monastery, he traveled to India, where he—"

The door opened and Jack entered the room, his ragged breathing giving evidence of the fact that he had run up to the fourth-floor nursery/schoolroom and back. He went immediately to the settee and resumed his seat beside Lydia, lifting the ends of his cravat just enough to show her something hidden inside his jacket. His manner was conspiratorial, and a youthful smile tugged at the corners of his mouth.

It had been months since Evan had seen his cousin act in such a boyish manner—since before the illness that had claimed his hearing—and it had been even longer than that since he had seen Jack smile. Whatever Miss Lydia Swann was up to, she would get no censure from Evan.

Captain Danforth chose that moment to ask Lydia if she would honor them by performing a selection or two on the pianoforte. "I love the sea," he said, "and I could not ask for a better life. But I must admit, one of the things I truly miss aboard ship is music."

"I assure you, Captain Danforth, you do not miss the sort of cacophony I produce. Besides," Lydia continued, "I promised Jack that I would sketch Lord Trent's likeness."

Evan did not miss the twinkle in those green eyes, nor the snicker his cousin attempted to hide behind his hand. *"My* likeness?" he asked. "Why would anyone want a picture of me?"

"To record the moment," Lydia said slowly, looking not at Evan but at Jack. "So that one day your cousin may look back on this day and remember you just as you were."

When she held her hand out to the lad, palm up, he unbuttoned his jacket and removed a sketch pad that was yellowed with age. Evan recognized the pad immediately. It contained pages that bore longitudinal and latitudinal lines, the sort of paper he had used years ago when his tutor had required him to draw maps of the world for geography assignments.

After taking the sketch pad, Lydia tapped Jack on the wrist, then pointed to a brace of candles on the pianoforte. Immediately, the boy understood what she wanted and hurried to move the candles to the mantel, close to where Evan stood.

"Now, sir," Lydia said, opening the sketch pad to a clean sheet, then turning it on its reverse side where there were no lines, "if you will be so good as to remain as you are for two minutes, I will take your likeness."

"Two minutes! Nonsense, madam. No one can take a likeness in that length of time."

"Nonetheless, please do as I ask. Stand still, and no talking."

With pencil in hand, she began to sketch, her movements quick, yet flowing, and while she worked, Jack and Michael stood behind her, looking over her shoulder. At first their faces were earnest, almost solemn; within a matter of seconds, however, the seriousness gave way to smiles. Occasionally, Captain Danforth would laugh outright, but no matter how indignantly Evan protested, demanding to know what was so funny, no one said a word to him.

Finally, Lydia held up the sketch so her auditors might see it properly.

"Perfect," Michael said, not even trying to hold his laughter in check. "I vow, ma'am, you have captured him to a nicety."

Unable to stand it another minute, Evan strode over to the settee and took the sketch pad from Lydia's unresisting hands, turning it so the candles gave him plenty of light by which to judge the drawing. To his surprise, it was not a portrait at all, but a caricature. With but a few deftly executed lines, Lydia had constructed his face in profile, and though she had drawn his jaw and chin so square they resembled a box, and his eyebrows so bushy they put him in mind of a pair of hedgerows, there was no denying that the person depicted was Evan.

Lydia had drawn a patch over the one eye, and given him a tricorn, the hat bearing the skull and crossbones of a pirate, perhaps in honor of the fictional privateer, Lord Timothy Tambour. As for the slightly exaggerated ears, and the overly long nose, Evan doubted Lord Tambour would appreciate those appendages any more than *he* did. He was about to protest when Michael said, "It bears a striking resemblance to you, old boy. Definitely your chin."

With that, Jack burst out laughing.

The instant Evan heard the boy's laughter, he swallowed his words of censure. Jack was taking part in a social gathering, something he had not done in weeks, and he had even gone so far as to fetch the sketch pad for Lydia. That in itself was something to be celebrated, but there was more. Jack had laughed. If Lydia's drawing could make the boy so forget himself as to laugh aloud, then Evan was prepared to frame the blasted caricature and hang it in the picture gallery between the priceless Holbein and the treasured Rembrandt.

If Lady Trent could have known Evan's thoughts, she would have heartily endorsed her son's plan. She had returned to the drawing room while their guest was busily sketching Evan's likeness, and rather than intrude upon the scene, she had chosen to remain quietly by the door. Now, with the sound of her nephew's happy laughter still echoing in her ears, moisture filled her eyes, obliging her to search in her reticule for a handkerchief.

As she dabbed at the tears that spilled down her cheeks, Lady Trent offered a prayer of gratitude to Heaven for sending them Miss Lydia Swann. By some stroke of magic, the slender, red-haired young woman had managed what neither Mary Trent nor her son had been able to do. For a moment, at least, Lydia had transformed a sad, self-conscious youth into the smiling boy he had once been.

Her prayer completed, Lady Trent vowed to find some way to show her gratitude to the conjuror of such dear magic. After a moment, the perfect idea occurred to her; she would do all within her power to help Lydia capture the heart of the gentleman of her dreams.

Of course, it would not be wise to act precipitously, and under no circumstances must Lydia be rushed. After all, she was an intelligent young lady; if given enough time, she might decide that the face that had previously filled her dreams was no longer right for her. And who knew? If a new face replaced the old, the new one just might bear a small scar across the left eyebrow.

Five

"Actually," Lydia said above the steady rattle of the curricle wheels on the hard-packed earth, "I know almost nothing, only what Uncle Milford showed my sisters and me. As for my success with Jack last evening, I merely employed what little I know, and relied on a young boy's natural wish for society to carry the day."

"And it did," Evan said, the quiet words spoken more to himself than to her.

Evan had chosen to drive the matched grays today, and they were moving along at a steady trot, one that should see Lydia delivered to Osborne Grange in slightly more than an hour. As the curricle traveled through the village of Alderbury, with its half-timbered shops and cottages, then continued down a lane that bore the characteristic straightness of an old Roman road, they passed rich farmland to their left, while to their right red cliffs, thick gorse, and woodland glades abounded, providing startling scenic contrast. The trees had begun to display their autumn colors, and while Evan admired the bright golds and oranges that touched the tips of the leaves, his traveling companion continued to speak, though Evan had offered no further comment.

"About fifty years ago," Lydia said, "the Abbe de

L'Epee founded a school for the deaf in Paris. In his teachings, he employed finger spelling as well as a form of sign language used by the early Christian monks who had taken vows of silence. The signs I showed your cousin last evening were probably not that different from those taught at the Abbe's school.''

Evan looked down at the young woman beside him. She was not normally such a chatterbox, and it occurred to him that she might be experiencing a bit of nervousness over her coming reunion with Sebastian Osborne. Not that Evan minded her chatter. If the truth be known, at this moment he was prepared to give Lydia Swann the moon if she should ask for it.

Apparently she had no idea that what she had accomplished last night was a minor miracle—one that promised to be permanent. To Evan's surprise, Jack had joined his cousin and his aunt for breakfast this morning, something he had not done since before his illness.

The lad had entered the small, sunny morning room, nodded briefly, then gone to the mahogany sideboard to select his breakfast from among the half dozen covered dishes. After taking his place at the oval table, Jack ate without attempting to communicate with Evan or Lady Trent, but at least he had remained with his family until everyone had finished their meal, only then returning to the solitude of his bedchamber.

Evan was more grateful than he could say, and to show his gratitude to the instigator of last night's miracle, he was prepared to assist Lydia in her pursuit of her heart's desire, driving her to the Grange every day if that was her wish. Now, as Evan studied the pert little nose that showed just the tiniest hint of freckles, and the thick brown lashes that rested against Lydia's flawless complexion, he wondered if Sebastian Osborne had the least notion that he had won a prize, won it without even trying.

And Lydia was a prize. Her beautiful sisters, with their blond hair and their well-turned figures, might be considered diamonds of the first water, but Evan was beginning to suspect that Miss Lydia was the pearl of great price.

As if the lady had felt him staring at her, she turned to look at him, a question in her lovely fern-green eyes. "What is it?" she asked. "Have I a smut on my face?"

"Not at all. As always, madam, you are as neat as a pin."

"Then why do you look at me as if you wanted to say something that I might not like?"

Unwilling to tell her that he had been weighing her beloved Sebastian's right to so great a prize, Evan said the first thing that came to mind. "I merely wondered if you would teach me a few of the signing words."

"Of course. If you like. Though they are not words per se, but concepts. Uncomplicated things like, 'Pass the salt' or 'Come this way.' Nothing earth-shattering; just simple, everyday ideas."

"I see. And if the occasion should arise, how would I ask for . . . the salt, for instance?"

"Nothing easier." To demonstrate, she reached out in front of her, pinching her thumb and fore-finger together as though taking a bit of salt from a cellar; then she rubbed her fingers back and forth as if sprinkling the seasoning over a plate of imaginary food.

"The difficult part," she added, "might be getting the attention of the person sitting closest to the salt."

"I see your point. That could be a problem."

"And before you ask," she said, a smile playing upon her full pink lips, "tossing a bun at the fellow's head is not an option."

Evan chuckled. "I should think such tactics were not common practice among the brothers of the monastery. Of course, I have no idea what customs prevail when the Swann family are at table."

"Not bun tossing," she informed him. Then, after a slight hesitation, "At least, not lately."

"Madam, never have I heard a remark that begs explanation more than 'Not lately.' "

"While still in the nursery, I *may* have tossed a bit of food at the twins from time to time. But you must understand, sir, they were such lovely toddlers, with their big blue eyes and their silky blond curls. Surely you can see what an irresistible temptation it was to add a bit of gooseberry jam to their tresses."

"Tell me you did not!"

She sighed, the sound exaggerated. "I am very much afraid I did."

Evan tried not to laugh. "Did you, er, decorate your sisters very often?"

She shook her head, causing the jaunty feather atop her jasper-green silk bonnet to sway in the breeze. "Not *too* often."

"Tsk, tsk, madam. Had you no shame?"

"None whatsoever. Not having any siblings of your own, sir, I cannot expect you to understand the depth of jealousy a four-year-old can feel when obliged to share the nursery, the nanny, and the parents that were once hers alone. To the difficulty of surrendering one's place as an only child, add the rarity of twins; then stir in a pair so beautiful that even strangers felt compelled to comment upon them, and you will have a situation in which a skinny little red-haired child might feel obliged to spread a bit of jam.

"Of course," she added, "I came to love my sisters in time, especially when they grew big enough to join me in games of hide-and-seek or boating on our little pond."

"Boating? Surely that was an unusual recreation for little girls."

"Perhaps, but I have always loved the water. We used to spend hours playing on the small quay or rowing about in my little punt."

Apparently recalling one of those idyllic occasions, she smiled.

"Twopence for your thoughts," he said.

She hesitated only a moment. "I used to pretend the punt was a sleek racing shell, like the ones Uncle Milford told us about from his days at Oxford. Shells that sped up and down the Thames, manned by young men in colorful team caps with numbers sewn on their bills. I would make the twins row for hours while I sat in the stern, counting cadence like a coxswain directing the crew. It was great fun!"

"Fun for whom, you little tyrant? You or the poor twins who did all the rowing?"

"All three of us, actually. Clorinda and Clarissanne are not very imaginative, so they always fell in with whatever I suggested. They never seemed to mind, even when it earned them an occasional dunking in the pond."

"I trust you and they could swim."

"Why, of course," she said, a teasing light in her eyes. "We are Swanns, after all."

Evan groaned at the pun, but his companion merely laughed.

"Madam," he said. "Since I am no admirer of low humor, I am happy to inform you that we have arrived at the Grange."

She sat up very straight, all amusement gone from her face, and stared at the break in the hedgerows just to their left. If nothing else, while she had talked of her childhood, she had forgotten about her nervousness. Now, Evan saw her take her bottom lip between her teeth as if to stop it from trembling.

Without further conversation, they turned onto the short, well-tended carriageway and headed directly for the manor house. At least three centuries old, the black-and-white half-timbered building was magpie architecture at its most exuberant, rambling and unapologetically homely.

"There it is," Lydia said. "Just as I remembered it." She got no further, for the entrance door swung open and a blond girl of about thirteen came running out. Evan could only stare, for the girl was as pretty as a picture, and she resembled Clarissanne and Clorinda enough to be their sister rather than their cousin.

To his further amazement, the smiling girl was followed from the house by a lad perhaps an inch taller than she. He, too, was blond, and his face was a masculine version of the girl's.

"There are my cousins," Lydia said, waving her

arm above her head. Evidently noticing Evan's confusion, she said, "Did I not tell you? Twins run in my mother's family."

"Cousin Lydia!" the boy yelled. "Is it really you?"

While Evan reined in the horses, then turned them over to the groom who came running from the stables, Lydia greeted her cousins. "Bernard! Barbara! Hello to both of you. How marvelous to see you. Is . . . Is my aunt at home?"

Though Lydia made the inquiry with all sincerity, Evan had no difficulty hearing the question she did not ask, the one he knew most concerned her: was their stepbrother, Sebastian, in residence?

"Mother is here," Barbara replied, "but Papa James and Sebastian are from home at the moment. They are in London, at one of Tattersal's auctions, purchasing a horse. Then they are to stop off at the home of Papa James's sister, Mrs. Fieldhurst, to fetch her and her daughter and bring them to the Grange for the big birthday celebration."

A horse! Lydia wanted to scream her frustration. *How could Sebastian be purchasing a horse at such a time? As for Penelope Fieldhurst, why would anyone waste precious time stopping off for that whey-faced little crybaby?*

As Lydia allowed Evan to assist her from the curricle, she tried to hide her disappointment at the news. If the truth be known, she had been more than a little nervous about seeing the gentleman whose handsome face had filled her dreams for the past eight years. Even so, only twelve days remained before she must return to Lower Dewes, and it was frustrating to discover that Sebastian was not at the Grange.

Postponing their reunion meant that one of those

precious days was wasted. As well, it meant that Lydia's uncertainty was prolonged. Though she had worn her most becoming ensemble—the jasper-green hat and matching silk spencer—she still worried that Sebastian might not find her attractive enough to win his heart.

Whatever her uncertainties, Lydia was obliged to put them aside for the moment, for Barbara had hugged her with typical Hilton exuberance, and Bernard was now following suit, showing off his strength by lifting his cousin off the ground and swinging her around.

"Put me down, you impertinent puppy! Have you no respect for your elders? What will Lord Trent think of us?"

Bernard Hilton set Lydia on her feet; then without the least embarrassment, he turned to Evan and bowed. "How do you do, sir?"

"Very well, youngster." Then, after making the girl a gallant bow, Evan said, "Miss Barbara, it is a pleasure to make your acquaintance."

The girl was as free of embarrassment as her brother, and after curtsying politely to Evan, she slipped her arm through Lydia's and began leading her into the house. "Mother will be so pleased to see you, Cousin." Before Lydia could respond, the chit whispered to her, though the comment was loud enough to be heard by the gentleman in question. "Never tell me," she said, "that you and Lord Trent are engaged. Is that why he has brought you here?"

"Actually, he—"

"Not that I should blame you, of course, for his lordship is quite handsome, in a rugged, piratical sort of way. Still, I always thought you meant to have Sebastian."

"Barb and I know some signs, too," Bernard said between large bites of seedcake. "Uncle Milford showed them to us."

"Yes," his mother said, "and the rudesbys use them all the time. I cannot tell you how provoking it is not to know what is being said."

"But, Mother," Bernard said, "do you not see? That must be exactly how Lord Trent's cousin feels. Jack, is it, sir?"

"Yes," Evan replied. "Jack Trent."

Lydia set her teacup on the small piecrust table situated between hers and her aunt's chairs. Like the inhabitants of the Grange, the rooms were warm and friendly, with no pretense about them, and though Minerva Hilton Osborne was stylishly dressed in a blue lustring frock that complemented her still-youthful figure, the brown velvet chair in which she sat was as comfortable and as unfashionable as an old shoe.

Pointing to the letter that lay in her aunt's lap, a missive bearing Lady Trent's signature, Lydia said, "If you mean to accept her ladyship's invitation to tea tomorrow, Aunt, I expect Barbara and Bernard can use their knowledge, rude though you think it, to communicate with Jack."

"*If* I mean to accept the invitation? My dear, I would not think of declining it. So kind of her ladyship to ask us."

"I assure you, ma'am, my mother looks forward

to making your acquaintance. Yours and your family's."

Their hostess sighed. "I pray Lady Trent will be of a like mind once she meets the pair of Gypsies you see before you. They have no manners at all, and what your lady mother will think of them, I vow I cannot even guess."

She turned to her niece. "Lydia, my love, if you have any influence with them, see if you can teach them to say, 'Please' and 'thank you.' "

"Of course, Aunt."

After winking at her cousins, Lydia patted her lips with her napkin and returned the linen to her lap. " 'Please' and 'I want' are the same gesture," she said. Then, with both hands out, palms open, she pulled her hands toward her, at the same time bringing her elbows back against her ribs. " 'Thank you' is conveyed with one palm flat, after which one touches the tips of the fingers to the chin and points to the person being thanked."

"My dear," her aunt said, "I had hoped you might show them how to *practice* good manners."

The lady's children burst out laughing, and after a moment she joined in their merriment, taking her niece's little joke in good part. "I see, my dear, that adulthood has not changed you. You still enjoy your little jests."

Lydia reached over and squeezed her aunt's hand. "Forgive me, ma'am. I could not resist."

If the squire's lady was unimpressed with signing, Evan was not. "Please," he said, "show me how to say Jack's name."

"An individual's name," Lydia explained, "is a

matter of personal choice. For myself, for instance, I sign my initial; then I touch it to my shoulder."

She demonstrated by closing her fist, then pointing her thumb skyward and her first finger forward. The letter made, she touched it rather quickly to her shoulder and said, "Lydia."

Evan followed her lead by making a fist, then pointing his thumb and first finger as she had shown him. However, instead of touching the letter to his shoulder, precisely as she had done, he touched it rather closer to his heart, letting it remain there for a matter of seconds. "Lydia," he repeated.

To his surprise, the gesture sent Miss Barbara into a fit of the giggles that she tried unsuccessfully to hide behind her hand. As well, a rush of color had invaded Lydia's cheeks. Uncertain what he had done to cause the two reactions, Evan turned to the only other male in the room. "Have I made a fool of myself?"

"No, sir. It is just that if you sign a person's name over your heart, it . . . Well, it means you love them."

"Aunt," Lydia said, changing the subject rather abruptly, "how did your roses fair this summer?"

The remainder of the time was spent discussing their hostess's garden, and in family reminiscences. When the visit was at an end, the boisterous Hilton twins followed Evan's curricle all the way to the end of the Grange carriageway; then they stood in the lane waving their arms above their heads and yelling farewells until the vehicle was out of sight.

The send-off, though a bit unconventional, was so genuine that Evan could find no fault with it. Besides, he liked the twins. He could picture Lydia at their age, and in his imagination she was not unlike her cousins, intelligent, full of energy, and overflowing with a love for life.

Not that Lydia was exhibiting any of that energy at the moment; in fact, she was unusually quiet during the drive back to Trent Park. For the next hour, she offered only monosyllabic responses to such conversational gambits as Evan threw out, while she introduced not one topic for discussion. Evan assumed her preoccupation was due to disappointment at having missed seeing Sebastian Osborne. He could not, of course, ask her about something so personal, so he kept his questions to himself.

If the truth be known, Evan was happy the squire and his son had not been at home today. He was beginning to think he might not like Mr. Sebastian Osborne; though his prejudice might well have something to do with the fact that everyone who knew the Greek god seemed to believe him perfect in every way.

Once, when the ladies had gone abovestairs to refresh themselves, and Bernard and Evan were alone, Evan had asked the boy how he liked having a stepbrother.

"Sebastian?" Bernard asked, as though the question had surprised him. "Who would not like having such a brother? You must know, sir, that Sebastian is top-of-the-trees. A real go amongst the goers."

"I see."

"And yet," the boy continued, his exuberance unabated, "Sebastian never acts top-lofty, or comes the ugly. Why, when he is at home, and I ask if I may accompany him while he shoots or while he rides about the estate, he never tells me to get lost just because I am a schoolboy."

"Laudable," Evan remarked, attempting to keep the sarcasm from his voice.

"Furthermore," Bernard added, obviously not convinced that their visitor truly appreciated the magnitude of Sebastian's virtues, "my stepbrother rides like he was born to the saddle. He's positively fearless when riding to hounds, for there was never a horse foaled that Sebastian would not throw his leg over, nor a fence or a hedge too high for him to jump."

If Evan thought such behavior sounded rather more like recklessness than fearlessness, he kept his opinion to himself.

"And Sebastian can shoot to an inch. He has little interest in swords, so he does not pursue fencing, but he's ever so handy with his fives. Why, once at Gentleman Jackson's Boxing Establishment, Sebastian milled down the champion."

"Milled down the champion, did he?"

"Yes, sir. Not that Sebastian bragged about it, mind you, for he's no Jack-a-dandy who can't wait to tell of all his accomplishments. He just happened to mention it once in passing."

"And your sister?" Evan said. "How did she adjust to having an older brother?"

"Barb? Why, m'sister positively adores Sebastian. Always has, from the moment our mother married Papa James. But then, all the females make cakes of themselves over Sebastian."

"Do they now? So he is a lady's man, is he?"

Bernard considered this for a moment. "I do not think so. He likes the ladies as much as they like him, but I do not believe he is more fond of one lady than the other. Or if he is, he has not mentioned it to Mother or to Papa James.

"Of course," he added, "the men like Sebastian, too, him being so good at sporting pursuits and having such an agreeable, easy-going nature. You'll see what I mean when you meet him, my lord. I am persuaded you and he will get along famously."

Evan took leave to doubt it. For some reason, each time he heard Sebastian Osborne's name, Evan liked the fellow a little bit less.

Six

"I wish I could tell you," Lydia said, making certain Jack was looking at her when she spoke, "that if you chose to go about in society, no one would ever stare at you or make impertinent comments. Unfortunately, I can make no such assurances."

Noting the lad's disappointment, she added, "No one is exempt from occasional rudeness and hurtful behavior. Not even the members of the royal family. At least when you drive to the theatre, no one throws overripe vegetables at you, which is more than can be said for one or two of the royal dukes."

She and Jack sat on a stone bench situated to the right of a handsome bronze sundial that took pride of place in the center of the rose garden. They had sat thus for about an hour, signing a little and occasionally resorting to pencil and notepad, but mostly just enjoying each other's company and the warmth of the sun. It was a delightful place, for though the roses were long gone from bushes and trellises alike, the beech trees in the background remained full and green, their topmost leaves only just now showing a hint of the dramatic reds and golds to come.

"All I can tell you for certain," Lydia said, "is that if you remain sequestered here at Trent Park, you may avoid the occasional hurt inflicted by strangers, but you cannot escape completely the disappointments and the tears that come to all mortals."

She paused a moment to allow Jack to assimilate what she had said. "A recluse does, however, forfeit all chance of experiencing life to its fullest. Life, with its joys, its triumphs, its friendships, and its passions."

She smiled, noting the boy's averted eyes at the mention of passion. "Personally," she continued once he looked at her again, "I should hate to miss a single day of life. And I should dislike of all things to come to the end of my allotted three-score years and ten never having known love's fulfillment."

Jack scribbled hurriedly on his notepad. *Who would love me?*

"Who would love any of us?" she replied. "No one. Not unless we give them the opportunity. First, though, we must make their acquaintance. If we wish to find that one person who will love and respect us, and whom we can love and respect, we must seek them out. You may believe me when I tell you that soul mates do not drop out of the sky like gentle raindrops."

Lydia said nothing more for a time, certain she had given the boy enough to ponder for one day. She understood his family's desire to shield him and to allow him time to become accustomed to a silent world. To someone suddenly cast into a world without sound, everything was frightening. Things happened all around a person—potentially dangerous things—yet unless the person was looking directly at the occurrence, he was totally unaware that he was not alone. How terrifying that must be!

And yet, regardless of his fear, Jack needed to begin living again. With the help of the twins, Lydia hoped today would prove to be the day Jack made the commitment to rejoin the world.

Lydia had promised to teach the lad a few more signs before the twins arrived, so that he could communicate with them. He was understandably nervous about meeting Barbara and Bernard; not that Lydia blamed him. She was far from calm herself, for there was a slight possibility that Sebastian might accompany the party.

The visitors from Osborne Grange were due to arrive some time after the noon hour, and as the thin shadow cast by the verdigrised arm of the sundial crept closer to twelve, Jack became more fidgety. He had not been in company with a boy his own age since his illness, when he was sent home from Eton, and as far as Lydia knew, he had never been in company with a young female his own age. Even if he had, chances were the girl had not been as beautiful as Barbara Hilton.

Barbara's looks could present a problem. Lydia hoped not. Unfortunately, having grown up with the lovely Clarissanne and Clorinda, Lydia had noticed on more than one occasion that even the most confident of males were apt to misplace their brains when in the presence of a beautiful female.

To still Jack's and her own anxieties, Lydia gave them something else to think about by placing her hand over his and pushing his thumb beneath his first and second fingers. "N," she said. "Now make a circle, with the tip of your thumb touching the tips of your first and second fingers. That is the letter 'O.' You may use that negative reply to any who would plague you with impertinent questions."

After Jack formed the two letters as he was instructed, he reached for his pencil and pad. *I still say, a bunch of fives to the nose would be more effective.*

Lydia laughed. "But, sir, what if it is a young lady who asks the impertinent question? In that instance, I assure you, a simple 'no' would be the preferred answer. Who can tell, she might have a truly large brother with a fist of his own."

Jack nodded; then after a moment's thought, he wrote, *Is Bernard taller than me?*

It was a such a typically male inquiry that Lydia was obliged to school her lips not to smile. "I cannot be certain. However, when my cousin arrives, I will make a point to see which of you is taller."

As it happened, Lydia had no more than made the offer when she heard carriage wheels rattling over the crushed stone of the carriageway. She touched Jack's wrist. "They are here," she said. "Do you remember how to greet them?"

Jack did not reply. He either did not realize that she had asked a question, or he was too tense to understand what she had said. Either way, he stood, his thin shoulders pushed back and his head up, as if he were being led to a French tumbrel, his destination a bloodied guillotine.

Lydia wished she could say something to calm his fears. If the truth be known, she wished someone would say something to calm *her* fears. Would she see Sebastian today? She had but eleven days left in which to convince him that they were meant for each other. Would it be enough? Could she convince him?

She had no more than asked herself that question when another one occurred to her: where was Evan? He was such a reassuring man to have around in times of stress, and Jack might feel more confident if his cousin was near.

As if the wish was mother to the deed, Lydia looked up to find Evan waiting at the entrance to the garden. He did not look at her or Jack; instead, he studied a cloud in the distant sky, his hand cupped above his brow to shield his eyes from the sun. He stood quietly, his long legs spread apart as if to maintain his balance on the deck of a wave-tossed vessel.

Watching him now, Lydia imagined Evan Trent had stood thus thousands of times when aboard ship, observing the sky for signs of tempestuous weather. In the short time she had known him, Evan had seemed so much the country gentleman, in his beautifully tailored clothes and his perfectly starched cravat, that Lydia had nearly forgotten he had spent his youth as a rough-and-tumble sailor.

And yet, with the sunlight upon his bronzed skin and a slight breeze ruffling his dark hair, he was so relaxed, so attuned with the elements, that Lydia could easily picture Evan in shirtsleeves, with the collar of the slightly dampened linen open to allow a sea breeze to cool the strong, work-warmed column of his throat. To Lydia's dismay, imagining him thus sent a frisson of excitement through her body.

It was a surprisingly intoxicating image, and Lydia felt slightly giddy, almost as if she had spied upon Evan in the privacy of his bedchamber. Thankfully, he could not read her mind, for he smiled when he saw them approaching, and when they drew near, he offered Lydia his arm.

She accepted the offer as graciously as possible, considering this new, and rather disturbing impression of Evan that had taken hold in her mind. Without a word, she slipped her hand through the crook of his elbow and along the sleeve of his corbeau green coat, allowing her fingertips to rest on his muscular forearm.

At the feel of that unexpectedly hard arm, Lydia experienced the oddest little flutter in the pit of her stomach. Odd, because she had not realized that a nervous reaction—which this must surely be—could be so pleasurable.

Dismissing the sensation, though not without some difficulty, Lydia walked between the two Trent men as they followed a beech-bark footpath around to the front of the house, where the squire's smart black and gold landau was already pulled up to the entrance. They arrived in time to see the butler bowing to Minerva Osborne and her son and daughter. Of the lady's relatives by marriage, there was no sign, and Lydia felt the disappointment like a blow to the heart.

Sebastian, if you only knew how much I wished you were here.

This entire trip had been undertaken so Lydia could display to the fullest the charm and social graces she had acquired in the years since Sebastian had seen her last. But how could she show the gentleman anything if he did not come to see her?

On the chance that he would come to Trent Park today, Lydia had arranged her coppery tresses in their usual neat twist atop her head, but she had allowed the maid to apply a heated curling iron to the wispy hair at her temples. The effect of the soft curls framing her face had been most gratifying, and Lydia had been eager to see Sebastian's reaction.

Her sigh did not go unnoticed by the gentleman in the corbeau coat. "Relax," he whispered close to her ear. "Trust me, you look quite charming." An instant later he added, "By the way, I like the curls."

The warmth of Evan's breath upon the surprisingly sensitive skin near her earlobe had sent a delicious little shiver through Lydia, and though his compliment should have made her feel more confident about meeting Sebastian, it had just the opposite effect, prompting a return of those little flutters in her midsection.

Thankfully, Evan seemed unaware of the strange responses going on inside Lydia, for his attention was claimed immediately by the new arrivals—Mrs. Minerva Osborne in a stylish carriage dress of Clarence blue, and Miss Barbara Hilton in a sprigged muslin whose pale pink flowers matched the ribbons of her chip-straw villager hat.

Evan bowed to the ladies, personally pleased to see that they were accompanied only by Bernard, and not their other relatives. Mrs. Osborne was all smiles, and for once, the boisterous twins, both of whom appeared to have brought pencil and pad, stood quietly, waiting for the necessary introductions.

"Aunt Minerva," Lydia said, after saluting the lady's cheek, "Lord Trent you know, but may I present his cousin, Mr. Jack Trent?"

"How do you do?" she said, offering Jack her hand.

The lad bowed politely, taking the gloved hand Mrs. Osborne offered. Next he bowed to the lady's daughter, then to her son. Apparently, it was only when Jack lifted his eyes that he got his first real look at Barbara Hilton—a look that all but turned him to stone. Not that Evan blamed him. Even at the tender age of thirteen, the chit, with blond curls cascading down her back, was a stunner.

At the moment, the young lady, apparently unaware of the effect she had on Jack, was smiling candidly at him. As he continued to stare at her, she lifted her hand, the first three fingers pointed sideways, then made an arc from her chin to her sternum. At the same time, she said, "Hello, Jack."

As if suddenly realizing that he was imitating a stone pillar, Jack blushed; then he reciprocated Barbara's sign and said rather haltingly, "W-welcome."

It was a simple greeting, no more than any other boy might have said; except that Jack Trent was not any other boy. Jack had not spoken before a stranger in months, and at the sound of the boy's voice, Evan felt his throat constrict with pride at his young cousin's courage.

During his years as a naval officer—years in which his ship and crew had faced numerous French ships, the enemy canons firing, their intent to kill as many English as possible—Evan had seen enough young men swallow their fear to know bravery when he saw it. At that moment, it was all he could do not to give his cousin a hug to show him how proud he was of his pluck. He did not touch him, of course; instead, he acted as though Jack greeted guests every day.

"Mrs. Osborne," Evan said. "Miss Barbara. Bernard. Please, come inside. Lady Trent is eager to make your acquaintance. And I wish to make you known to our other houseguest, my oldest and dearest friend, Captain Michael Danforth."

It was not to be wondered at that Barbara and Bernard could not maintain their show of decorum for more than the thirty minutes required to take tea in the formal blue drawing room. Once the half hour was accomplished, and Bernard Hilton, the only one of the young trio who appeared unaffected by the occasion, had consumed a heroic number of tiny sandwiches, plus a spun-sugar basket filled with glazed apricots, and one or two cream cakes, he used the toe of his boot to give Jack's boot a brief kick. When he had the boy's attention, he said, "What do you say we walk down to the river?"

"Oh, yes," Barbara said, rising. "I should love to see the river."

It was unclear if Jack understood what Bernard had said, but the moment Barbara stood, Jack was on his feet, apparently ready and willing to follow the pretty blonde to the very ends of the earth if that was her destination.

"The very thing," Lydia said, rightly interpreting the concern on Lady Trent's face, "for I have been longing for a closer look at the river. If I may, I will join you presently."

"Yes," Michael Danforth said. "You three go ahead. If Miss Swann will allow me to escort her, the two of us will make the trek down later."

Later proved to be another full half hour away, and by the time the captain and Lydia made the

slow, but pleasant descent down the Italian-style terraces that led to the shallow tributary of the Mersey
River, the three young people were fast becoming
friends. Little wads of used notepaper littered the
shaded ground beneath a thick-branched beech
tree, giving evidence of the many messages already
exchanged between the three, and both boys had
removed their jackets and loosened their cravats, the
better to show each other their prowess at tree
climbing.

"Cousin Lydia," Barbara called, causing the swans
that floated nearby to turn and paddle away, and
sending the red-crested grebes into a frenzy of loud
craerr, craerr, crearrs. "You missed the show, Cousin.
Not ten minutes ago a racing shell passed by, the
two oarsmen wearing the Cambridge colors."

"There is to be a race meet this Sunday afternoon," Bernard added, "in honor of the fifth anni-
versary of Lord Nelson's victory at Trafalgar. The
oarsmen are practicing for the event."

Smiling her prettiest smile, Barbara asked, "Do
you suppose we could go to the meet?" After glanc-
ing quickly toward Jack, the chit returned her attention to Lydia. *"All* of us?"

"Splendid idea!" the captain said. "Do you not
agree, Miss Swann?"

Lydia gave it as her opinion that it was a fine idea.
"However," she added, "I cannot speak for Jack or
for his cousin and Lady Trent."

"As to that," Captain Danforth said, "if our host
is otherwise occupied, Miss Swann, there is no reason I cannot escort you. That is, if you should not
dislike it."

"Famous!" Barbara said, not giving her cousin an

opportunity to respond to the captain's invitation. "You being a naval man, Captain Danforth, you can bring us up to date on all the nautical terms."

"Yes," Evan said, surprising Lydia by his sudden, unannounced appearance just behind them, "terms like backstabbing pirate or unmitigated blackguard. Terms which I regret to inform you, Miss Barbara, perfectly describe the type of fellow who comes to another man's home, pretending to be his oldest friend, then at the first opportunity betrays him by making off with all the pretty ladies."

Captain Danforth merely laughed at the intended insults. "For those of us who have dedicated our lives to the sea, pretty ladies are few and far between. Surely no one can find fault with a poor sailor not wasting a minute of his limited time ashore."

Evan muttered something beneath his breath. "Poor sailor, indeed! Does that taradiddle still garner sympathy for you, Michael?"

The captain merely smiled, and since Barbara was busy scribbling something on her pad, and handing it to Jack, who nodded in affirmation, Lydia thanked the naval gentleman for his offer of escort to the race meet. "You cannot know it, Captain, but I have always wanted to see a race meet, for I love the water."

"And I, Miss Swann, have always loved *ladies* who love the water."

Evan watched this interplay with something less than enjoyment. Michael was, of course, making a cake of himself, only Lydia did not seem to notice. A person could be forgiven for thinking that a lady who had come all this way with no other purpose in mind than to secure the affections of a certain gentleman, would rebuff the attentions of any *other* gentlemen.

Since the lady was even then laughing at something else outrageous the captain had said, Evan was obliged to admit that Lydia had no intentions of offering Michael a rebuff. He was wondering if he should give his old friend a hint, when Jack took that moment to thrust his notepad in Evan's face, asking if he might attend the race meet.

Evan, more pleased than he could say at the lad's wish to partake of a bit of society, put aside all thoughts of his flirtatious friend and gave it as his opinion that they should all make a day of it. "What say you, Lydia? Would an al fresco nuncheon be in order?"

A smile lit her face. "I would say, sir, that it needed only an al fresco nuncheon to make the outing perfect! How like you to think of it."

Actually, it was not like Evan at all, for he detested eating out of doors. Furthermore, he had no idea where the suggestion had come from; it just seemed to pop out of his mouth, possibly a result of his annoyance with the captain. Whatever its source, the invitation was made and could not be rescinded, and with Lydia smiling at him as though he had promised a rare treat, Evan decided he would be a fool not to give al fresco dining another try.

By the time Lydia returned to the drawing room, having left Evan and the captain at the river with Jack and his new friends, each trying to outdistance the other in skipping rocks across the water, Mrs.

Osborne was drawing on her gloves in preparation to depart.

"Oh, Aunt," Lydia said, "must you leave so soon? Jack and my cousins are having such a nice time."

"Unfortunately, my dear, I fear we must go. This has been a most enjoyable visit, but the squire and Sebastian are surely returned to the Grange by now, and wondering where we have got to. At least I hope they may be at home, for the clouds are gathering, and the sky is beginning to look quite threatening."

"Indeed it is," Lady Trent agreed, "and though I should love to encourage your aunt to remain another hour or so, I have lived in this neighborhood long enough to know how quickly the weather can turn. Gentle rains can become torrents within minutes, turning country roads into quagmires and making travel all but impossible."

"But it is the fog I fear most," Minerva Osborne said. "It rolls in so quietly that it takes the unwary by surprise."

Lady Trent nodded in agreement. "I cannot recall how many stories I have heard of hikers becoming lost in the fog. Out for an afternoon's scenic ramble along some seemingly innocent mountain path, the unsuspecting hikers do not notice the fog until it is too late, at which time they are obliged to take refuge for the night in some sheepherder's hut."

"If they are fortunate enough to find such a hut," her visitor added. "Why, about this time last autumn, a trio of hikers were lost for two days, huddled against the side of the mountain, afraid to move for fear of falling to their deaths!"

Such dire stories being indisputable, Lydia sent a footman down to the river to fetch her cousins, and within a matter of minutes, good-byes were exchanged all around, and the Osborne party was climbing aboard their landau.

As it transpired, the weather did change, and by dinnertime the rain was coming down in earnest. After the gaiety of the afternoon, the evening seemed rather quiet, and Lydia asked Lady Trent if she might be excused from tea so that she could write some letters to her family. Her hostess readily agreed, then excused herself as well, claiming interest in a novel newly arrived by mailcoach from town. With the two ladies both abovestairs, Evan and the captain were left to entertain themselves and soon retired to the games room for an evening of billiards.

At Trent Park, the games room was a large and pleasantly masculine place, with walnut wainscoting adorning the lower half of the walls and a dark-red flocked paper above the wood. Comfortable leather chairs flanked the stone fireplace, where a cozy fire had been lit to ward off the evening chill. At the top of the room, identical drop-leaf card tables stood against the wall, while an ornately carved billiards table took pride of place at the bottom of the room.

Normally Evan would have liked nothing better than a few hours spent in his friend's company. On this particular evening, however, his enjoyment was seriously hampered by something he had overheard Barbara Hilton whisper to Lydia that afternoon as the two had said their good-byes.

"Lydia," her cousin had said, the words audible to Evan, who stood close by, "Captain Danforth seems in a fair way of falling in love with you. I am persuaded that if you but smiled at him, and looked deeply into his eyes, he would make you an offer."

"Barbara, for Heaven's sake! Must you marry me to every gentleman you meet?"

Undaunted, the irrepressible chit had added, "I would take him if I were you, Cousin, for he is quite the most charming man I have ever met."

"And you have met so many?" Lydia had asked. Not waiting for a reply, she gave the younger lady a decided shove into the coach.

Now, with that overheard conversation fresh in his mind, Evan was remembering how attentive his old friend had been to Lydia on more than one occasion, and he decided it was time he told Michael about their guest's real reason for coming to Alderbury.

Having missed the red ball entirely, Evan took the chalk cube and began to coat the tip of his cue. "You know," he began, while Michael prepared to take his turn, "Mrs. Osborne has a stepson."

"You don't say so?"

As Michael aimed and shot, his cue ball caromed off the cushion, hit Evan's cue ball with a soft click, then hit the object ball, causing it to speed across the green baize to come to rest in the corner. Satisfied with his point scored, he said, "Well, if the fellow is anything like young Bernard, and that saucy minx, Miss Barbara, I shall look forward to meeting him. Will he be at Sunday's race meet, do you suppose?"

Evan shrugged his shoulders. "I cannot say. For the past few days, Sebastian and his father, Squire Osborne, have been in town purchasing a horse at Tat's. They are, however, expected to return at any moment." He paused while Michael took his next shot, connecting with the object ball once again. "For Lydia's sake," Evan said, "I sincerely hope Sebastian has returned in time for the races."

Michael looked up, replying quietly, "For Miss Swann's sake? Are you telling me the wind is in that corner?"

"Afraid so, old fellow. Lydia has been in love with Sebastian since she was only a year or so older than Miss Barbara."

Over the years, Michael had vowed more than once that he planned never to marry, but at the news of Lydia's *tendre* for another man, his gray eyes seemed to lose their usual sparkle. "Ah, well," he said, after a moment, his voice uncharacteristically quiet, "being a sailor's wife is not a fit life for any female."

"True," Evan agreed. "It is not."

Michael seemed not to hear. "Though I wager if anyone could make a go of it, it would be Miss Swann. A more pleasant young lady I never met. And pluck to the backbone. Both good qualities for a sailor's wife. And," he added with a sigh, "she likes the water; she told me so."

As if giving the lie to his imperturbable tone, Michael took his next shot and missed without coming anywhere close to the object ball. "When I first arrived," he said, "I rather thought that *you* and Miss Swann were—"

"No, no. Nothing like that, I assure you." Evan walked around to the other side of the table in search of a more advantageous angle for his shot. "I admire Lydia, of course. Who would not? But like you, I have no wish to marry."

"Never said I had no *wish* to marry, old boy. Simply did not think it a good idea. Not as long as I was at sea for ten months out of the year. But I must admit that I wonder sometimes what will be my lot once I retire from His Majesty's navy. No wife. No children. No chance at grandchildren. It sounds a rather lonely existence, don't you think?"

Surprised at his friend's serious tone, Evan said, "Surely it is early days for that sort of reflecting."

"Perhaps. But like you, I am already turned thirty. A man cannot wait forever, don't you know, or all the superior females will be taken."

When it was Michael's turn to shoot again, he chalked his cue, though his attention appeared no longer on the game. "I have often wondered what sort of man would choose to spend his life alone." He paused, seeming to mull over his own question. "Not a man in his right mind, I should think. Especially not if he had even the smallest chance of securing the affections of someone like Miss Lydia Swann."

Seven

It sounds a rather lonely existence, don't you think?

Later that evening, Evan lay upon his bed, watching the flame from his bedside candle cast a dancing shadow upon the far wall. While he listened to the sound of rain hitting the windowpanes, and the occasional roll of thunder in the distance, Michael's words replayed themselves in his head. *What sort of man would choose to spend his life alone? Not a man in his right mind, I should think. Especially not if he had even the smallest chance of securing the affections of someone like Miss Lydia Swann.*

What sort indeed?

Of course, Evan had already formed the opinion that Lydia was too great a prize for Sebastian Osborne, but for the life of him he could not say why he had turned his face against Michael's possible suit. There was no basis for such disapproval of his old friend. True, Michael Danforth was not a wealthy man, but his lineage was good, his naval career was distinguished, and his character was without blemish.

A woman could do worse than marry a man of Michael's stamp. Especially a lady like Lydia, who was no longer in her first blush of youth, and who possessed little or no dowry. And yet, Evan had been annoyed by his old shipmate's attempts to secure Lydia's attention. Not that he blamed Michael overmuch, for Lydia was so full of life, and so completely natural—a bit of a madcap, but without a pretentious bone in her body.

Unlike many females who were only happy when in the midst of society, dressed in the height of fashion and covered in jewels, Lydia appeared unimpressed by worldly possessions or social status. If she had been desirous of obtaining those objectives, she would have snapped up a wealthy and well-connected peer like Evan Trent when she had had the opportunity.

Lydia had not taken him, of course. In fact, she had not even considered holding him to that stupidly worded proposal letter. Instead, she had devised this plan to renew her acquaintance with Sebastian Osborne, a mere squire's son, and in so doing, she let Evan off the matrimonial hook.

Now, instead of counting his blessings that he had not been caught in parson's mousetrap, Evan lay there gazing at the shadows on the far wall and recalling how Lydia had smiled at Michael that afternoon, when they were at the river's edge. She had even told him of her love for the water. Evan remembered, as well, Michael's flirtatious reply—that he loved *ladies* who loved the water—For some reason, the memory so irritated Evan that he yanked one of the pillows from behind his head, and using his fist, proceeded to pound the downy contents into shape.

It felt good to pound something! Amazingly good!

Not that he had any reason to be angry with his old friend. It was just that Evan had known Lydia the longest, and he felt that by right she should have turned to *him*, should have laughed with *him* as she had laughed with Michael, with her eyes bright and her pretty mouth parted and inviting.

Inviting? Of what? A kiss, perhaps?

Yes! A series of kisses actually.

At the thought, Evan fancied he could almost feel that series of kisses, and so vivid was his imagination that a pulse began to beat in his neck, the clear, rhythmic sound echoing in his ears. Without realizing he did so, he held the pillow against his chest and closed his eyes.

In his mind, he drew Lydia's slender body ever closer to his, and when he felt the warmth of her breath upon his face, he bent his head and covered her soft lips with his own. He could feel her shy, yet warm response; sense the passion newly awakened in her. As if she were really in his arms, he experienced the thrill in store for them both as he taught her the mysteries of—

"Damnation!"

He sat up, eyes wide open. What the deuce was he thinking? And how had such wayward thoughts taken possession of his brain?

Cursing again, Evan threw the offending pillow across the room.

Actually, it was not too difficult to guess what was wrong with him. It was an all too common complaint among sailors and other men who went for months without the comfort of a bit of female companionship. Evan needed to go to town, where he might seek out some beautiful barque of frailty whose scented embraces would ease this unsettling feeling he had been experiencing for the past few days.

That was it! That was the solution. How foolish of him not to have thought of it sooner. A quick trip to town for a brief liaison would cure what ailed him.

Happy to have discovered what was bothering him, and even happier to have arrived at a suitable plan of action, Evan blew out the candle, then settled comfortably against the remaining pillows, his hands behind his head. It was a good plan, simple and easily carried out, for when the month of October was ended, and their guest was either engaged to Mr. Sebastian Osborne or returned to her home still unspoken for, Evan would take himself up to town for a fortnight or so and forget he had ever met Miss Lydia Swann.

It should require little effort to forget about her. After all, how hard could it be to erase from his memory that captivating sprinkle of freckles across her nose? As for her eyes, it should be a simple matter to put all recollection of those intriguing green orbs from his mind. And surely it would prove no trouble at all to obliterate completely all thought of those damnably kissable lips.

If Evan had difficulty falling asleep, the same could not be said for Lydia, who finished her letter to her parents, then crawled beneath the covers. Though exhausted by the continued strain of having to wait for Sebastian to return, she was soon lulled to sleep by the hypnotic sound of the rain, and to her delight, she awoke the next morning feeling rested and surprisingly optimistic about the success of her remaining ten days' stay in Alderbury.

"T'rain be gone, miss," said the young maid, who had brought up a small tray bearing a pot of fragrant hot chocolate. "It ended some time last night. And Heaven be praised, it took t'thunder and lightning with it." She shuddered. "I'm that afeared of lightning."

The servant drew the window hangings aside so Lydia could see for herself the happy reappearance of the sun. It was, indeed, shining, and it sparkled on the green hills in the distance, making them appear like so many giant emeralds. "T'land be drying out already, so it should be a fine day for t'race meet tomorrow, though there still be mud aplenty in t'lane today."

Since a muddy lane would preclude any traveling between Trent Park and Osborne Grange, Lydia knew she would not see Sebastian this day. Somehow, though, just knowing that there was no possibility of it, and that any decisions had been taken from her hands, allowed Lydia to relax. She would not see Sebastian today because she *could* not see him—Nature had decreed it—and not being the type to mope overlong about things that could not be helped, Lydia set her mind to enjoying the company already in the house.

Actually, if a person was obliged to be housebound, she could not ask for better companions. Lady Trent was a gracious and undemanding hostess; Jack was a thoroughly likeable lad; and Captain Danforth was as charming a fellow guest as Lydia could hope for. As for Evan, after an inauspicious beginning, he and Lydia were in a fair way of becoming friends.

Evan was proving to be a most cooperative co-

conspirator in her plan to reunite with Sebastian, driving her to Osborne Grange in his curricle, then inviting her relatives to Trent Park. Though a squire's family would not generally move in such exalted circles, Evan had not hesitated in opening his home to the Osbornes and making them feel welcome.

But then, Evan was not the least bit starched up. Evan Trent never displayed any of the haughtiness one might expect from a viscount of his wealth and lineage. True, Lydia had thought him a bit aloof when she had first met him, but that was understandable, for at that time he was concerned about being forced into an engagement he did not want. Since then, however, he had shown none of his earlier reserve. He was, in fact, a most agreeable gentleman, and he was fast becoming one of her favorite people.

An intelligent and well-educated man, Evan could speak knowledgeably on a number of topics, and he never condescended to Lydia because she was a female. Any time she ventured an opinion on a subject, he listened attentively, showing her the same courtesy and respect he showed Captain Danforth. In fact, Evan had a way of looking at her when she spoke, his attention never leaving her face—a way that made her feel as though she was the only person in the room.

"You want I should set out your dress, miss?"

"What?" At the maid's question, Lydia remembered that she was not, in fact, the only person in her bedchamber, so she put aside her recollection of Evan's warm brown eyes in favor of selecting a suitable frock to wear belowstairs.

Some thirty minutes later, attired in a pretty pale-yellow muslin her mother had brought her from Bath, Lydia entered the small cream-and-green morning room, where an informal meal was laid out on the mahogany sideboard for those who wished to break their fast. At the moment, Captain Danforth was the only person seated at the oval table, and the only sound in the room was the occasional scrape of a knife and fork across the surface of a China plate.

At Lydia's entrance, the captain looked up; then, with a smile of welcome, he set aside his cutlery and rose from the table, making an elegant bow. "Good morning, Miss Swann."

"Please," she said, returning his smile, "do not let me disturb your meal."

"Disturb? Impossible, ma'am, for you are a veritable ray of sunshine."

Crossing to the sideboard, he took a plate from the stack, handed it to Lydia, then began lifting the lids of the covered dishes so she might make her selections. "I see you are an early riser."

"Very true. I enjoy the morning hours."

With the air of one accustomed to paying compliments, the captain said, "I need not ask if you slept well, for the roses in your cheeks and the brightness of your eyes give evidence of a salubrious night's repose."

Lydia chuckled at the ridiculously gallant remark. "Flattery so early in the day, Captain? I am beginning to suspect, sir, that yours is a golden tongue. The sort that gives credence to the stories one hears about sailors having a sweetheart in every port."

"She has found you out," said a voice from the doorway.

Lydia turned to find Evan standing just behind her. Freshly shaved, and dressed in a beautifully cut burgundy coat that perfectly suited his dark hair and bronzed skin, he was so handsome that Lydia found herself wondering how many broken hearts *he* had left in his wake.

As if discerning her thoughts, the tall gentleman gave her one of his rare smiles—a smile that did something to her knees, causing them to weaken momentarily.

"You are very perceptive," he said. "As for Michael's history, I can attest to the fact that he has left a string of weeping maidens from Portsmouth to Madagascar."

"Here now!" the captain said. "I protest such defamation of my character."

"Sorry, Danforth, but the truth will out. When a man travels the world, charming all the ladies into falling under his spell, he cannot expect to keep it a secret forever."

"Surely you do not speak of me, old boy?"

"Who else?"

"And what of yourself? Why, I remember once when we stopped in Gibraltar for a sennight, and you—" He paused, obviously recalling just in time that the two old shipmates were not alone. "Beg pardon, Miss Swann. Boring stuff, this."

"Not at all, Captain. You see me quite fascinated. Pray continue with your story of Gibraltar."

"Minx!" Evan said, coming forward and taking the still-empty plate from Lydia's hand. "As for you,

Michael, pray *discontinue* with all conversation concerning my misspent youth.

"Instead," he added, elbowing his old friend aside, "allow me to tempt the lady with a few of Cook's specialties."

Without waiting for permission, Evan placed upon Lydia's plate a more than generous portion of braised kippers, following that with two coddled eggs. "Now," he said, a definite hint of retribution in his eyes, "allow me to serve you a slice of ham, and two or three of those delicious-looking flaky things."

Lydia turned away before Evan could make good his threat to serve her some of everything on the sideboard, and made her way to the table, allowing Captain Danforth to seat her. "Is it not a beautiful day?" she asked, introducing a topic that would earn her no more unwanted food.

"It is that," the captain agreed.

"Unfortunately, my maid informs me that it is still too muddy to venture out of doors."

"In that case," the gentleman said, "we must do what we can to keep ourselves entertained while confined to the house. What say you, Miss Swann? Will you entertain us later with a bit of music? Or perhaps another caricature?"

"If you wish, sir. However, I had hoped for a different sort of activity. That is, if you would not find it a dead bore, Captain, to share with me a bit of your expertise."

"I should be honored, ma'am. Though I confess I cannot call to mind a single talent of mine that would be of the slightest interest to a lady."

"Nor I," agreed Evan, who had taken a seat across

the table from Lydia. Giving her a suspicious look, he said, "Furthermore, when I recall some of the childhood misadventures you have described to me, among which were using your younger sisters like galley slaves, then tipping the boat so the poor poppets fell into the water, I positively tremble at the thought of the sort of activity you might wish to pursue while confined to the house."

"Galley slaves! I say, Miss Swann, what have you in mind for us?"

"Nothing so very threatening, Captain, I assure you. I should merely like to learn to play billiards."

"Billiards!" both men said at once, surprised at such a request from a lady.

When Lydia remained adamant that she wished to learn the game, the gentlemen fell into a friendly argument that lasted for most of the meal, their objective to decide which one of them was the properest person to undertake the lady's instruction.

"You would be well advised to choose me, Miss Swann. Modesty prohibits me from boasting of the number of times I have bested Evan at the art, but—"

"Bested me? And where was *I* during those so-called victories? Asleep?"

"Weeping in some corner, more like, considering the amount of money I have earned at your expense."

"Gentlemen," Lydia said, trying not to laugh. "I beg of you, let us have no more of this . . . er, reminiscing. I am persuaded there will be more than enough opportunity for both of you to instruct me."

"No, no," Evan said. "Just as too many cooks spoil

the broth, too many instructors would be bound to turn you against the game forever."

While the argument raged, Jack Trent entered the morning room, filled his plate, then joined the trio at the table. At first, he appeared more interested in his food than in what was being said, but after a time he passed Lydia a note, asking her what they were discussing.

I am to be instructed in the game of billiards, she wrote. *Would you care to join us?*

At his enthusiastic nod, it was decided that Captain Danforth would undertake to instruct Lydia, while Evan saw to his young cousin's education. "And we shall see," Evan said, "just who bests whom."

The battle lines drawn, the foursome soon retired to the games room, and the lesson began.

"Billiards," Captain Danforth said, "is played with two white balls and one red." He showed Lydia and Jack that one of the white balls had two small, colored dots on it. "The dots distinguish it from the other white ball, and if this is our ball, Miss Swann, then the other one belongs to our opponent and is, along with the red, an object ball."

Lydia nodded to show her understanding. "And my goal is to hit both the object balls?"

"Exactly, ma'am. At which time, you will score a carem, or point."

After ascertaining that Jack understood the rules, Evan chalked a cue stick and showed the lad how to line up his shot. That done, he demonstrated how a point was made. By hitting the cue ball precisely, with just the right amount of force, the ball struck one of the object balls, bounced off three separate cushions of the table, then struck the other object ball. "There," he said slowly, "we now have a carem."

"A carem," Jack repeated.

Eager to try his own skill, the lad took the cue stick from Evan, and after carefully studying the green baize surface of the table, he slid the wooden cue between his fingers a few times to get the feel of it; then he hit the cue ball. Naturally, he did not strike either of the object balls, for doing so was not as easy as it looked. Still, after a few tries, he had come close enough to the object balls to feel encouraged.

Since good sportsmanship demanded that he let Lydia have a few tries, Jack stepped back and allowed their guest sufficient room to maneuver around the table. She, too, found the game more difficult than it appeared, and after a time she asked the captain if she was holding the cue stick properly.

"Perhaps you are holding it a bit too tightly, ma'am. Try, if you can, to relax."

Because neither Jack's nor Lydia's arms were as long as a full-grown man's, the two beginners were obliged to lean farther across the table than was common. Of course, Evan had barely noticed the circumstance when his cousin was practicing his shots, but when Lydia took her turn, the situation was quite different.

The lady was not wearing a fichu over her shoulders, and though the neckline of her pale yellow dress was not unconventionally low, when she bent to line up her shot, a surprising amount of her small, creamy-white bosom was exposed to view. Naturally, Evan did not look away immediately—not until he noticed that his young cousin's attention had been captured as well.

After giving the boy a nudge on the shoulder, then scowling at him in a way that needed no words, the cousins took themselves around to the other side of the table, out of temptation's way. Unfortunately, Evan had not given thought to what the view might be from the other side; not until Lydia bent again. This time, it was the young lady's pretty derriere that was displayed, and so temptingly exhibited that Evan found it necessary to run his forefinger beneath his cravat, which had grown so tight it threatened to choke the life from his overly warm body.

"Here," he said, taking the cue stick from Lydia's hands. "Let me show you."

Assuming it would be better for him if he was close enough so he could not ogle his guest's figure, Evan positioned the cue stick between his fingers, then showed her how to slide the wood back and forth without tightening one's grip.

"Now you try," he said.

When she still had difficulty, Evan decided it would be easier to demonstrate if he guided her hands. Again, he discovered his error too late!

Stepping behind her, Evan stretched both his arms along the length of her slender arms, then pressed his palms gently against the backs of her hands, curving his fingers around hers, which were in turn, curved around the wooden cue.

At the unexpected contact, the lady tensed, her body almost as rigid as the cue. "Relax," Evan said.

"I-I am trying," she replied, the words spoken rather shyly for the usually intrepid Lydia Swann.

"Take a deep breath," he said. "Then let it out slowly. That usually does the trick."

It did something right enough! As far as Evan was concerned, however, it failed miserably as a relaxation technique.

While Lydia slowly filled her lungs, Evan discovered that he could feel every movement of her delicate frame, and the discovery awakened all his senses. By the time she exhaled, he had moved that fraction of an inch closer to her, and was obliged to use every last ounce of his control to stop himself from slipping his arm around her waist and drawing her even closer. Slender she may have been, but Lydia Swann was all woman, and she fit perfectly in his arms.

And she smelled wonderful! All fresh and clean and feminine, and before he could stop himself, Evan had leaned his head close to hers and breathed deeply of the slightly floral scent of her hair.

Heaven help him! He had never smelled anything so intoxicating. If he did not do something immediately, he would be in trouble. Unfortunately, he knew for a fact that he could *not* do the thing that was running through his fevered brain. No point in imagining how easy it would be to turn Lydia in his arms so that she faced him, or how by simply putting his finger beneath her chin and lifting her face, he could claim her lips.

"What now?" she asked.

"Now?" he repeated, bemused. "Why, I—"

"Now," Michael answered for him, "you concentrate on the object ball." Then to Evan, he said, "I think Miss Swann has the idea, old boy. It would be

a good thing if you stepped back and gave her room to shoot."

Calling himself all kinds of a fool, Evan released his hold on Lydia then stepped back several paces, all the time wondering what had come over him to make him behave in such a manner.

Later, when he and Michael were alone, enjoying a glass of brandy in the book room, his friend asked him that same question. "What the deuce were you thinking, old fellow, pawing the lady about in that manner?"

"I was not pawing her."

"Right. And I have never been to sea." Michael took a sip of his brandy, then set the glass on the table beside his chair. "Must I repeat the warning you issued to me last evening, old fellow? Must I remind you that Miss Swann is in love with another man?"

Eight

Evan had no idea how his guests had entertained themselves following the billiard lesson. Thankfully, there had been some estate business that wanted seeing to, giving him a reason to absent himself from the house. Even so, for what remained of the day, he had been unable to remove from his thoughts the memory of how Lydia had felt in his arms, and how badly he had wanted to kiss her. Convinced that it would be best if he avoided her for a while, he stayed away until it was time to dress for the evening meal, thereby managing not to see the lady again until the party gathered in the blue drawing room prior to dinner.

When he entered the room, Lydia and Michael were sitting on either side of the fireplace, enjoying the cheery blaze. "Jack and I spent the afternoon in the nursery," he heard her telling Michael, her tone so cheerful that Evan could only assume she had not given him a thought since the episode at the billiard table.

"The nursery," Michael repeated. "And if I may ask, ma'am, what sort of activities occupied your time there? Nothing too scandalous, I trust. No silver loo at a guinea a point, or high-stakes faro?"

"Nothing so exciting as all that, Captain. Jack and

I merely beguiled the hours by playing such childish games as Fox and Geese and Pope Joan."

Michael threw up his hands, pretending to be shocked. "Oh, ye defiler of youth."

Lydia chuckled. "Perhaps I will not be totally sunk in your estimation, sir, if I relate that after tea, we forsook those more infantile pursuits in favor of a game of chess."

"Vastly relieved to hear it, ma'am. Dare I ask who won?"

"I am happy to inform you, Captain, that I still hold the championship for Fox and Geese."

"And Pope Joan?"

Lydia ducked her head in feigned modesty. "I hate to brag, truly I do, but I was victorious there as well."

Michael laughed at her theatrics. "And the chess match? Never tell me you trounced the lad in that as well."

"I can tell you no such thing, sir, for Jack took the honors there. He is a very bright young man. And unlike me, he thinks before he acts."

Evan sincerely hoped it was true that his cousin thought before he acted, for not half an hour before he came down to dinner, Evan had received a note from the lad, a folded paper that had been slipped under the door while Evan dressed for the evening meal.

Crossing to the drinks table, Evan recalled the brief message.

Cousin,
    Regarding the subject of matrimony, I have reconsidered my position, and I believe I will wed after all.

I know my change of heart will meet with your approval, for now you will be relieved of the burden of seeking out a wife for yourself.

Yr. Obt. Servant
Jack Trent

Reconsidered his position had he? Too bad he had not done so *before* the havoc was wrought. But for the lad's original declaration to remain single, Evan would never have written that ill-advised letter to Sir Beecham Swann, asking for the hand of his eldest daughter. And had Evan never gone to Swannleigh Manor, he would not now be bound by his promise to aid Lydia in her quest to become Mrs. Sebastian Osborne.

"Ah, Evan," Michael said, spying him at last, "there you are. Just the man I wish to see."

"Really?" Evan said, not bothering to hide the sarcasm in his tone. "Had anyone asked me, I would have said you were too engrossed in joking with Lydia to give a thought to anyone else."

Lydia's cheeks turned pink, but Michael chose to ignore his host's surly reply. "Actually," he said, "I was wondering if you had an argon lamp about the place. One sufficient to the task of casting shadows for silhouettes."

"Silhouettes?"

"Yes. Miss Swann has been so gracious as to agree to draw silhouettes of each of us."

"I can do so following dinner," she said. "If a lamp is available."

"There is such a lamp in the book room. If you like, I will have one of the servants get it and bring it to the drawing room."

"Thank you," she replied quietly.

Later that evening, when it came time for the execution of the silhouettes, both Captain Danforth and Lady Trent professed themselves far too interested in their newly devised version of whist to wish to stop.

"Do Evan first," the captain suggested.

"Yes," Lady Trent said. "Be so good, my dear, as to begin with my son."

With no valid reason to refuse their request, Lydia bid Evan come with her to the far end of the room, where a chair had been placed in a darkened corner before a blank wall. A large square of white drawing paper had been affixed to the wall, and when Evan was settled in the chair, Lydia positioned the argon lamp so the light from it shone on his head, casting a sharp shadow on the paper.

"If you will," she directed, "move just an inch to your right, for your silhouette must be in the center of the square."

Evan did as she bid him, but the new position was too far in the other direction, causing his shadow to go off the edge of the paper. "Now, a bit to your left," she said.

When that move proved too drastic as well, Lydia was obliged to position Evan's head herself. After placing her hands on either side of his unsmiling face, she guided him just the least bit forward, lifting his chin ever so slightly until his entire image fit the paper to perfection.

"Thank you," she said, her voice none too steady.

Lydia had not wanted to touch him. It was the last thing she would have chosen to do; for ever since that morning, when she had been so foolish as to ask to be taught the game of billiards, the idea of touching Evan had not been far from her thoughts. Or more to the point, the thought of his touching her.

What sort of person am I to entertain such thoughts?

In the past few hours Lydia had asked herself that question at least a thousand times. She had never considered herself a flirt, and certainly the idea that she might prove to be fickle hearted had never entered her mind. For eight years she had been true to Sebastian, wanting nothing but an opportunity to see him again and convince him that they were meant for each other. And now, when that dream was within her reach, she was suddenly entertaining thoughts of another man's arms around her.

When Evan had come around the billiard table to show her how she should hold the cue stick, Lydia had been unprepared for his method of demonstration. He had stepped behind her, and even before he touched her, she had felt the aura of his strength. Then, without warning, he had aligned his muscular arms with hers, and his strong yet gentle hands had cupped hers. Equally without warning, Lydia's heart had begun to pound, and every inch of her skin had come to life with awareness of Evan Trent.

"Relax," he had told her. Yet how could she?

She had often wondered how it would feel to be in a man's arms, but until that moment she had not known it would rob her of her reason. Nor make her yearn for things she could not even name.

"You took the trick!" the captain shouted from the far side of the drawing room, and though he spoke to Lady Trent, his voice recalled Lydia to the present. "And I made sure you had no more trumps in your hand."

"I warned you how it would be," Lady Trent replied. "I play to win. Now shuffle the pack, Danforth, and let us get down to some serious play."

While the card playing began in earnest, Lydia put from her mind all thoughts of the billiard game and gave her attention to the silhouette. She used a freshly sharpened pencil to trace around the edges of Evan's shadow, being careful to follow the line of his profile as faithfully as possible. This was no caricature, and she wanted to do justice to his masculine, yet quite pleasing face. He might want to keep this effort; at least, she would like to think he might.

Even in shadow, Evan's features were strong, his jawline noticeably angular, and his hair thick and slightly wavy. Choosing not to include his shoulders, Lydia ended the neckline in a simple vee before outlining the back of his head, hesitating for some reason about tracing his hair.

She was being ridiculous, of course, for she had lifted Evan's chin earlier to guarantee the proper position for the silhouette. Still, a degree of trust was required before one person allowed another person to touch his head, and Lydia felt that to touch Evan, even in shadow, without asking permission implied an intimate relationship. Or at the very least, an invasion of his privacy.

Either way, Lydia's hands trembled as she completed the tracing and removed the paper from the wall. "Now," she said, hoping her voice did not betray her confusion, "I will cut your image from the white paper, transfer it to the black, then cut it again. Once the black cutout is completed and affixed to a piece of white pasteboard, the whole can be trimmed to fit any frame you wish to use. That is, if you feel it worthy of framing."

"I shall frame it," Evan said quietly.

The simple statement left Lydia feeling slightly breathless. Hoping Evan would not notice her foolish reaction, she tried for a teasing reply. "A rash promise, indeed, sir. Perhaps you should wait until you have seen the finished product. You might consider it too amateurish by half."

"I shall frame it," he said again.

To Lydia's surprise, he said no more, simply bid her a good evening, then turned and strode from the room, without offering a word to his mother or to Captain Danforth.

Sunday dawned every bit as bright and sunny as Lydia had hoped for, and after the party from Trent Park attended services at the village church, with its glorious fifteenth-century woodcarving and its Jacobean pulpit, they returned home to change into clothing more suitable for attending a race meet. Lady Trent begged to be excused from further racketing about, explaining that she felt a headache coming on, so at one of the clock Lydia and her three male escorts climbed aboard her ladyship's landau and set out once again for the village.

Alderbury had been chosen as the site for the race because the portion of the Mersey that flowed past the village was nearly straight for the required one mile. Evan had disabused Lydia of the notion that this was merely a local meet when he informed her that hundreds of spectators were expected, some of whom would come from as far away as London. "They will be lined along both banks of the river for the entire mile," he said, "with scarcely an inch to spare."

Surprised, Lydia asked, "Will there be room for us?"

Evan nodded. "Actually, the most advantageous spot for viewing the competing boats is on a privately owned knoll about a quarter of a mile north of the village. The competition will begin about half a mile downstream of the knoll and continue for another half a mile upstream, making that the perfect vantage point."

"And we can go there?"

"We can," he said.

Since Evan had seen fit to send a request to the farmer who owned the land, plus a ten-pound note for the man's trouble, the party from Trent Park had been assured an excellent spot for viewing the race, as well as for their al fresco nuncheon.

He told none of this to Lydia, however, for her attention had been captured by the throng of people who had overrun the small village, making travel particularly hazardous. Banners hung from every conceivable shop sign and window, proclaiming the race meet and the commemoration of Admiral Horatio Nelson's glorious victory at Trafalgar, and the flapping of those banners prompted more than one horse to rear up in protest. As well, there were at least two dozen carriages crowding the narrow high street, the drivers searching in vain for the best place to set down their passengers.

Adding to the congestion were at least a hundred

sporting gentlemen who sauntered about, greeting friends, placing bets, and amusing themselves by ogling any pretty girl who happened to pass by. There were men of lesser pedigree as well, and like the gentlemen, they eagerly awaited the time to take their places along the river banks.

Lydia had never before seen such a crowd, and after witnessing the rudeness exhibited by some of the other carriage drivers, many of whom were unsuccessful in finding a space wide enough to accommodate their equipage, she quite agreed with Captain Danforth's evaluation of the scene.

"Whew!" he said. "So much humanity in one spot makes a man long for the vastness of the sea."

"Or the quiet of the country," she added.

In contrast to the village, the knoll, when they reached it, was comparatively serene, even though the Trent party did not have the space completely to themselves. Several other families had been allowed access as well, and they, too, had planned al fresco meals. While the servants of those families set to work arranging the tables and chairs, Evan took the opportunity to pay his respects to one or two of his neighbors.

Jack was understandably reticent to mingle with the other families, so he remained with Lydia and the captain, eagerly watching for the arrival of his new friends, Bernard and Barbara Hilton. As for Lydia, though she looked forward to seeing her cousins again, there was a tenseness in her as well, for something told her that Sebastian would be with the Hiltons today.

Since the meet was scheduled for two o'clock, and that time was drawing near, neither Jack nor

Lydia had long to wait for the arrival of the Osborne landau. Within a matter of minutes, the carriage rattled over the rough earth leading to the knoll, the landau's double hood let down to reveal four passengers.

Bernard and Barbara rode with their backs to the horses, while two young ladies Lydia did not recognize occupied the forward-facing seat. At first, she wondered who the young ladies might be, but before she had time to give their identity much thought, her entire attention was caught by the two men who followed on horseback. Or, at least, by one of the men.

Sebastian! He was here at last, and at the sight of him, Lydia began to tremble.

Heaven help her! He was even handsomer than she had remembered. Tall and slender, he rode a beautiful black horse, and the pair were perfection itself—the animal's coat blue-black in the sunshine, and Sebastian's blond hair shining like pure gold.

"Oh, my," Lydia murmured, the words escaping before she could stop them.

"Steady on," Evan said softly; when he had joined her, Lydia could not even guess. "Compose yourself," he added. "The fellow is a man like any other."

A man like any other! Lydia could not believe Evan's lack of perception, for Sebastian was not a man at all. He was a god. A marvelous, blue-eyed Norse god come down from Valhalla!

"Cousin Lydia!" Bernard called to her from the slowing carriage. "Look who is come home. Papa James and Sebastian."

"Stubble it, halfling," Squire Osborne called, his

ready smile taking the sting from his words. "Chances are Miss Swann has forgotten ever meeting me and my son."

Forgotten! What lunacy!

Lydia wanted to run to Sebastian, to throw herself upon his neck and assure him that she had forgotten nothing, and that she loved him now with the same fierceness as she had loved him eight years ago. She would have done so, too, except that Evan had taken her hand and slipped it through the crook of his elbow. And now, for some perverse reason, he was forcibly detaining her, squeezing her arm against his side, his muscular forearm holding her a virtual prisoner.

She tried to pull free. When she could not do so, she stared at her captor. "Evan! What are you doing? Let me go."

"Be still," he said, the whispered words an unmistakable order. "People are watching, and I will not have you become the subject of gossip."

Realizing the wisdom of what Evan said, Lydia remained where she was, content for the moment just to watch Sebastian as he dismounted and went to the landau to help the two unknown ladies alight.

"Lord Trent," Barbara said, after coming forward and giving Lydia a hug, "my mother sends her apologies to you and to Lady Trent, but her sister-in-law, Mrs. Fieldhurst, arrived Friday in company with Sebastian and Papa James, and she and Mama remained at home so they might go over the plans for Papa James's birthday celebration this coming Thursday."

Having delivered the required message, the irrepressible chit winked at Lydia, then lowered her voice so that she could not be overheard by the rest of the party. "But we have brought Sebastian with us, as you see, Cousin. And, of course," she added, her tone bland, "we have also brought Sebastian's cousin, Miss Penelope Fieldhurst, and her friend, Miss Susannah Blakesly."

Penelope Fieldhurst? Surely that sophisticated creature in blue was not the whey-faced little crybaby Lydia remembered from eight years ago.

But, of course, she was, and Lydia soon discovered that *she* was not the only person whose looks had improved with time. Miss Fieldhurst had shown the good sense not to grow as tall as Lydia, and she had put her weight to much better use, allowing it to round out her figure in all the right places, especially in the bosom. Even her strictest critic could no longer call her whey-faced, for though Penelope's complexion was still pale, it was flawless. Without a freckle in sight!

As for Penelope's friend, Miss Blakesly, that young lady was petite perfection. No more than five feet tall, and just twenty years old, she possessed dusky curls and thick-lashed brown eyes, and she was as pretty as she could stare. As it turned out, she was also a rather shy girl, with little conversation, and a want of spirit, but Lydia might have liked her well enough had the brunette not had the audacity to hang on Sebastian's every word, looking up at him adoringly, as though she could not get enough of gazing into his handsome face.

Not that Lydia could fault her for that! It was just that Lydia had been waiting for eight years, and here was Sebastian come at last, and this perfect little creature was there as well.

"Her grandfather is a mine owner," Barbara whispered, "and she is an heiress. With fifteen thousand pounds."

It wanted only that!

"She had her come-out this season," Barbara continued. "She was not presented, of course, and for that reason she did not travel in the highest circles of society. Even so, I heard Mrs. Fieldhurst tell Mama that Miss Blakesly's father has already refused nine offers for his daughter's hand. I need not tell you what Papa James is hoping for."

No. You need not.

Lydia tried not to let this news depress her too much. After all, her cousin had told her only what Squire Osborne wanted. Sebastian might have some entirely different goal in mind.

Truth to tell, he favored Miss Susannah Blakesly with no special attention, but treated her in the same careless manner he treated his cousin, Penelope—and Lydia, too, for that matter.

Always charming, Sebastian smiled, paid them all compliments, and divided his time equally between the three females. If Lady Trent had been there, he probably would have divided his time four ways. Not that Lydia blamed him for it. Sebastian could no more help being charming than he could help being a living, breathing Adonis.

"It wants one minute to two!" Bernard yelled, and he, Barbara, and Jack made short work of running to the top of the knoll.

The adults followed close behind, with the squire offering his arm to Miss Blakesly, and Michael stepping forward politely to partner Penelope Fieldhurst. Evan had stepped back several paces, his attention concentrated on something that seemed to be amiss with the heel of his left boot, so it fell to Sebastian to escort Lydia up the knoll.

"Miss Swann," Sebastian said, offering her his arm. "Shall we?"

Silently Lydia thanked Heaven for this unlooked-for moment alone with her beloved. As for thanking the gentleman, it seemed those words would be silent as well, for Lydia's mouth had gone so dry she could not force out so much as a sound.

Settling for a smile, she slipped her arm through Sebastian's, and the two of them strolled up the slight rise. At least the gentleman strolled; Lydia's knees shook so badly it was all she could do to walk upright. As for hearing a word Sebastian said, Lydia's heart beat so loudly she could not have heard the report of a cannon. Still, had she been offered all Croesus's gold, she would not have traded places with another soul.

At last she was exactly where she had always wanted to be. Beside Sebastian Osborne.

They reached the top of the knoll with only seconds to spare, just in time to see the twelve racing shells side by side at the starting point, their bows lined up perfectly, and their ten-foot-long skulls poised just above the clear blue water. Each shell held three men—the coxswain, who sat in the stern, and two oarsmen, all wearing the colors of their particular school or club—and all thirty-six competitors waited impatiently for the dropping of the flag, the sign that the race had finally begun.

There was a sudden hush, as if humans and birds alike had suspended even their breathing. Lydia did not see the flag drop, but suddenly a shout went up and all forty-eight thwartwise skulls dipped into the water, not a second's difference in their timing.

Above the din made by the spectators, Lydia heard the voices of the coxswains as they set the rhythm for their oarsmen. "Pull!" they shouted. "Pull. Pull."

And the oarsmen pulled. The dipped their skulls into the water at exactly the same moment as their teammates; then they lifted the oars out and repeated the process again and again. They never looked back, and they never looked to the side to see what the competition was doing. Instead, they listened for the coxswain and worked as a team, their muscles straining, yet their movements as precise and as graceful as those of ballet dancers.

By the time the two lead shells passed the knoll, Lydia had forgotten everything but her excitement over the race. At some point, she had released Sebastian's arm and stepped closer to the river's edge, and like the youngsters in the crowd, she was yelling her support for her chosen team. "Go, blues!" she shouted. "You can win. I know you can."

"Twopence says the golds edge them out," Evan said from just behind her.

Lydia had no idea when Evan had arrived, but she turned happily to accept the wager. "Twopence it is," she said. "Be ready to pay up the instant my blues cross the line as winners!"

As the shells neared the finish line, the blue team and the gold team had increased their leads, leaving the other competitors in their wake. The two lead shells were evenly matched, with first one bow moving ahead an inch, then the other bow coming alongside and moving ahead.

Only moments remained before the finish line was reached, with the blues ahead by no more than half a stroke. In the last two seconds, with the roar of hundreds of shouts spurring them on, the golds pulled from their depths one final burst of energy and moved ahead by a full stroke, crossing the finish line before their worthy opponents.

A deafening noise greeted their victory, and after the first wave of shouting subsided, Lydia turned to Evan, who stood just behind her. "Oh, Evan. Was it not a marvelous race?"

"Marvelous," he agreed.

"I vow, I could not have asked for anything any more exciting."

Evan laughed. "Except, perhaps, for your team to be victorious?"

"Naturally that," she agreed. "But the golds were wonderful, too, and I shall not begrudge them the win."

After one last look at the shells, which had all crossed the finish line and were even then turning about to drift back downriver to the starting point, Lydia sighed with pleasure. Recalling her bet with Evan, she removed her reticule from her wrist and began releasing the drawstring. "Twopence, you said?"

"Twopence," Evan replied. "And since it was you who set the rule, madam, I will have my pay on the instant."

"Here now," Sebastian said, apparently standing closer than Lydia had realized. "Surely, my lord, you will not hold Miss Swann to account." He laughed aloud at the thought. "You must know, sir, that females never mean it when they wager."

"Oh?" Lydia said. "And why is that?"

"Because you females do not understand the principle behind a debt of honor."

Lydia could not believe her ears. Did Sebastian think that she would go back on her word? How dare he make such an assumption about her. "I was not aware," she said, "that females were any less capable of honorable behavior than males."

Obviously surprised at her vehemence, Sebastian blinked. "I meant no offense, Miss Swann. Just stating a universally accepted fact."

Evan took no part in their conversation. Instead, he merely held out his hand toward Lydia, his palm up. "Twopence," he repeated. "On the instant."

Nine

The al fresco meal was a great success; that is, if a person's name was Penelope Fieldhurst. As for Lydia, the entire nuncheon, which she had anticipated with such pleasure, proved a disappointment. So much so, that the beautifully prepared food turned to sawdust in her mouth.

First and foremost, Sebastian sat on the opposite side of the makeshift table from her, making it impossible for Lydia to exchange more than the merest commonplaces with him during the endless meal. Then, to add insult to injury, Penelope had managed somehow to insinuate herself between Evan and Captain Danforth at the table. Not content with that piece of impertinence, however, she quite ruined Lydia's appetite by flirting outrageously with each gentleman in turn.

Not that the gentlemen seemed to mind. Especially not when the hazel-eyed she-cat had leaned forward more than was necessary, giving first Evan, then the captain an opportunity to view her ample bosom should they have wished to do so. And to Lydia's chagrin, they *had* wished to do so.

"La, Captain Danforth," Penelope crooned, running the tip of her finger along the square neck of her blue frock. "I grow positively faint just thinking about being on the ocean. The stormy winds. Those giant waves one hears about, waves tall enough to overturn even the largest ship." She shuddered dramatically. "I vow, you must lead the most exciting life."

The captain managed to pry his attention from the hussy's neckline long enough to reply. "Those giant waves are few and far between, ma'am, though we do get a bit of a blow from time to time. In general, however, a sailor's life is rather boring."

She gave him a wide-eyed stare. "Then, pray, why do you gentlemen all wish to go to sea? For my part, I would have you stay home and partner us ladies at the balls."

Lydia was already embarrassed that a member of her sex should make such an exhibition of herself, and now the twit had added to her transgressions by voicing a totally idiotic remark, particularly idiotic at an affair meant to honor the gallant Admiral Nelson. Unable to keep quiet, Lydia said, "A fine mess we ladies would be in, Penelope, if the sailors did stay home. Or do you fancy having Napoleon Bonaparte partner you at the next ball?"

Penelope gave Lydia a look that would curdle cream; then, without replying to Lydia's observation, she turned to Evan, her smile a fine blend of coquetry and witlessness. "I understand, Lord Trent, that you were a sailor, too. And quite the hero, as well."

"A sailor, yes, Miss Fieldhurst. As for my being a hero, I cannot lay claim to that designation. For such a man, you must look to the Navy's finest, Admiral Horatio Nelson."

"Here, here," Captain Danforth said, and the two

men lifted their wineglasses in memory of their fallen comrade.

To change the subject, Lydia asked the diminutive Miss Blakesly, who sat between Sebastian and the squire, if she had ever traveled to Alderbury before.

The dark-haired beauty nodded shyly, and though she looked up at Sebastian, as if beseeching him to speak for her, it was the squire who answered Lydia's question.

"Miss Blakesly's grandfather owns a copper mine not fifty miles north of here," he said, "and Miss Blakesly, Penelope, and my sister are to go on to the Blakesly estate after my birthday celebration." He smiled down at the young lady in a shamelessly obsequious manner. "We are honored that Miss Bla— Miss Susannah—was so kind as to stop off at the Grange, for my wife and I are become quite fond of her already. Quite like a second daughter."

The squire's comment could not have been more pointed, and Lydia wondered that Sebastian's face was not as red as the young lady's. To the contrary, Lydia's beloved appeared not to notice his father's broad hints and merely signaled to the footman to refill his wineglass.

Could Sebastian be that oblivious to his father's machinations to get his son a rich wife?

Lydia acquitted Sebastian of desiring to marry for money, for he was too fine, too noble a gentleman to be so materialistic, but she very nearly choked on a piece of fricasseed chicken when a new and thoroughly disturbing idea occurred to her. What if Sebastian's loyalty to his family prompted him to comply with his father's wishes?

He could not! Nay, he must not do so! Not when

Lydia loved him to distraction, had loved him for as long as she could remember. Fearing she might already be too late, she decided she must do something immediately to let Sebastian know the extent of her feelings for him. Otherwise, he might allow himself to become engaged to Miss Blakesly and her fifteen thousand pounds.

While Lydia was busy planning strategy that would enable her to be alone with Sebastian, Penelope asked Evan if he would escort her to the water's edge. "I long for a closer view of the river, my lord, but I fear I might miss my step and fall in." She shivered as though the water had already grabbed her and taken her under for the third time. "If I am to walk without trembling in fear, I need a gentleman's strong arm to ensure my safety."

To Lydia's dismay, Evan did not turn queasy at such drivel, but answered politely, "I should be honored, ma'am."

As soon as Evan pushed back his chair and assisted Penelope to rise, Bernard, Barbara, and Jack stood as well. The youthful trio, every bit as eager as Penelope to go down to the water's edge, but not nearly so fearful of falling in, asked to be excused. At Lydia's nod, they sped away, brother and sister yelling good-natured insults at each other as they ran.

"Last one there is a piker!" Bernard shouted.

"And that would be you!" his sister informed him, grabbing Jack's hand and racing ahead.

Thinking this as good an opportunity as any, Lydia took a page from Penelope's book and asked Sebastian if he would escort her. "Like your cousin, I should like a better view of the river."

"Happy to oblige," he said, and after bowing to Miss Blakesly, he came around the table and offered Lydia his arm.

They had not gone far when he leaned rather close to her ear, as if to ask her some private question. At the movement, Lydia felt a sudden acceleration of her pulse, and she held her breath, eagerly awaiting whatever intimate revelation the man she loved might wish to impart to her. "I say, Miss Swann, I believe you are the very person to answer something that has been on my mind this hour and more."

"Please," she said, all but lost in those gorgeous sky blue eyes, "ask me anything you wish."

"What is wrong with Lord Trent's cousin?"

Lydia was not certain she had heard Sebastian correctly, and for a moment her reply stuck in her throat. "Wrong?" she said finally. "With Jack? Nothing is *wrong* with him."

"I don't know. The boy seems a bit odd to me. Hope it is not a sign of some defect in the bloodline. If it is, I will need to hint Penelope away from Lord Trent, though he seems quite taken with her."

Astounded by Sebastian's lack of sensitivity, not to mention his suggestion about Evan and Penelope Fieldhurst, Lydia spoke more sharply than she would have liked. "Jack is not a bit odd, nor is his bloodline in question. And . . . and I will thank you to keep your prejudices to yourself."

Sebastian stared at her as though she had turned into some sort of two-headed monster. "Prejudices? Me?"

Realizing that she was wasting what little time she had with him, Lydia moderated her tone. "Forgive me for speaking so harshly, Sebastian. It is just that I am quite fond of Jack." Hoping to explain the situation, she said, "A recent illness left the lad unable to hear, a situation that has rendered him understandably shy with strangers. But aside from his lack of hearing, he is perfectly normal."

When Sebastian appeared unconvinced, Lydia continued. "Jack Trent is an intelligent and fun-loving boy, as my cousins have discovered for themselves. He is only just now regaining a bit of his confidence, however, so I beg you to be guarded in what you say. Jack does not need to hear any derogatory remarks."

"Thought you said he couldn't hear."

For Heaven's sake! Was Sebastian being purposefully obtuse?

"The boy has feelings," she said. "Surely you can understand that."

"Of course," Sebastian said. "No offense meant."

Sebastian had used that quasi apology before, and for some reason, it angered Lydia more each time she heard it. She longed to tell him, in the gentlest way, of course, that he should abandon the phrase, for it made him sound more flippant than repentant.

Thinking it wisest to keep that particular opinion to herself, Lydia was searching her brain for a subject that would prove less volatile, when Sebastian asked her if she had noticed the horse he rode today. "He is a recent purchase."

Heaven help her! Did men think of nothing but horses?

"Part Arab," Sebastian continued.

Not her father's daughter for nothing, Lydia knew what was expected of her. "He is a beauty," she said.

"That he is," Sebastian replied, his good humor instantly restored. Since he chose to bestow upon Lydia a smile so sweet it nearly robbed her of breath, she soon forgot her displeasure and allowed him to give her a rather detailed account of the various horses he had seen while at Tattersal's.

Long accustomed to her father's conversations, which generally centered on horses or hounds, Lydia was able to listen with only a portion of her concentration, uttering an occasional "Oh," or "My, yes," at the appropriate times. Meanwhile, she gave the majority of her attention to Evan and Penelope, who had stopped at the water's edge only a few feet away. Though Lydia abhorred an eavesdropper, she could not avoid being one, for the couple was close enough for the odd phrase or two to reach her ears.

"Yes," Evan said, "they have become fast friends in a very short time, and my cousin is quite fond of both Bernard and Miss Barbara. In fact, I was just thinking that with their mother busy with the plans for the squire's birthday celebration, perhaps we might take the two youngsters home with us for a day or two."

"La," Penelope said. "That is very generous of you, my lord. And quite a good thing for the twins, being in such exalted company."

"Nothing of the sort, ma'am, I assure you. The benefit is all on our side, having two such lively youngsters in our midst."

"Such modesty," Penelope continued, "and such condescension. I feel certain Uncle James will have no objections to the twins going to Trent Park."

Lydia would stake money on that certainty!

Penelope tilted her head in a manner that Lydia was certain the girl had practiced before her looking glass; then, after lowering her lashes for a moment, she raised her eyes, her gaze all but begging Evan for an invitation to his home. "The Park is, so I am told, the handsomest house in the whole of Cheshire."

Lydia blushed for the girl, who seemed to lack the sense to blush for herself. At least Lydia's blood relatives had not treated Evan in such a sycophantic manner.

"Marvelous bone structure," Sebastian said, reclaiming Lydia's attention. "And flawless withers. Prettiest filly at the auction. Still wish I could have purchased her."

"How interesting," Lydia replied. "Pray, tell me more."

While Sebastian enumerated the features of the horse he had finally chosen, Lydia strained to hear what Evan said to Penelope.

"We can take the two of them with us now," he said. "I feel certain the housekeeper can supply them with whatever personal items they will require."

"So good of you," Penelope murmured.

"Tomorrow," Evan continued, "or the day after, Mr. Sebastian Osborne may come to Trent Park to fetch his stepsister and stepbrother. He and Miss Swann are old friends, and I am persuaded they would enjoy an afternoon of catching up on family gossip."

Evan! How good of you to invent an excuse for Sebastian to come to see me!

"Sebastian?" Penelope said. "Fetch the twins? I cannot think he would do so, for he has little patience with youngsters and their prattle. Nor, for that matter would he find family gossip at all amusing. My cousin is far more likely to want to spend his day riding to hounds or out with my uncle shooting birds or hares."

"Of course," Evan added, albeit a bit hesitantly, "I had hoped that you might suggest to your cousin that he bring you and Miss Blakesly as well. I know my mother would be pleased if you would take tea with her."

Lydia could not believe Evan's generosity. He must know how particular such an invitation sounded, and Lydia could well imagine the fantasies taking shape inside Penelope's brain, fantasies about her becoming the next Lady Trent.

"Tea?" the she-cat purred. "With your mother? La, my lord. It would be an honor to meet Lady Trent, and I, for one, would not think of missing it."

Lydia did not doubt that for an instant! If nothing else, the visit to the Park, as well as Lady Trent's name, would most likely figure in Penelope Fieldhurst's conversation for years to come.

Evan's objective obviously accomplished, he mentioned something about it being time they returned home; then he called to the three youngsters, who were some distance away, motioning for them to come along. Since he and Penelope turned and began to walk back toward the carriages, Lydia heard no more of their conversation, and within a matter of seconds, she and Sebastian turned as well, following the other couple.

The leavetaking of the Trent party from the squire and his guests was protracted, and it would have taken even longer had Captain Danforth not grown weary and assisted both Penelope and Miss Blakesly into their carriage. Just before the landau pulled away, Evan bowed over Penelope's hand, leaving a brief kiss upon her fingers and prompting Lydia to wonder if his plan for Sebastian and his guests to come to the Park had truly been for *her* benefit.

If the truth be told, Penelope Fieldhurst was a pretty girl, if one liked the buxom, obvious type, and it was not inconceivable that the purpose of Evan's invitation had been so that *he* might see more of the hazel-eyed Penelope.

That question was still on Lydia's mind when the Trent party made their way to their own carriage. Earlier that day, during the trip to the village, her ladyship's landau had been a comfortable fit for Lydia and her three male escorts. With the addition of Bernard and Barbara, however, some adjustments had to be made.

"I will be happy to sit on the floor," Bernard offered. "That is, if Cousin Lydia will not mind me crowding her feet."

"She will not mind at all," Evan said, "for she will be sitting on my lap."

"What!" Lydia felt the heat of embarrassment travel from her face all the way down to her toes. *Sit on a man's lap? Penelope Fieldhurst might do such a thing, but not Lydia Swann. Any real lady's sensibilities would be offended at such a suggestion.*

As if he read her thoughts, Evan said, "I can understand your reservations, but it is the only sensible plan if we are to fit six into the landau. Unless, of course, you wish to see me run behind the carriage all the way to the Park."

Lydia shook her head. "Of course I do not. It is just—"

"*I* would certainly like to see you run behind the carriage," Captain Danforth said, a broad smile upon his face. "It would be a rare treat for those of us watching. Especially when one considers those handsome new boots you are wearing. Of course, I imagine a man of your excellent health would find a three-mile run quite refreshing."

Evan gave his old friend a telling look. "Perhaps we could both run. How is *your* health?"

"Or," the captain countered, ignoring his friend's question, "Miss Swann could sit on *my* lap. What say you, Miss Swann? The choice should be yours."

Lydia did not want to sit on anyone's lap, and she wanted even less to be given the dubious honor of choosing *whose* lap. "Captain, surely there must be some other way."

"You could toss a coin," Bernard said, adding his mite to Lydia's mortification. "That's the sporting way."

"Excellent suggestion," Evan said. As if to underscore his willingness to do the sporting thing, he reached inside his coat and pulled out the twopence he had won from Lydia earlier. "We will toss for the honor. Call it, Michael."

"Heads," the captain said.

Without another word, Evan rested the copper coin on his forefinger and flipped his thumb beneath it. The coin shot up at least two feet, spinning tightly as it rose, then fell to the ground.

Bernard bent quickly to retrieve the coin. "Tails,"

he said, handing the copper to Evan. "Cousin Lydia will sit on your lap, Lord Trent."

As if the matter were settled, everyone began to pile into the landau, and Lydia had no choice but to make the best of the situation. Actually, three miles was not so very far, and they would be at the Park in less than a half hour. What possible harm could it do to sit on Evan's lap?

The answer to that question came within a matter of minutes, for with Bernard taking up most of the floor space, Evan was required to reposition his legs every so often to keep them from going to sleep. Naturally, each time he moved, he was obliged to slip his arm around Lydia's waist to keep her from falling off his lap.

And just as naturally, each time his arm went around her, Lydia became more aware of Evan's strength, growing quite familiar with the feel of his thigh muscles bunching and relaxing. Unfortunately, the old adage proved incorrect, for in this instance, familiarity did *not* breed contempt.

In truth, Lydia was beginning to anticipate those position changes, even going so far as to close her eyes to block out all other sensations save the feel of Evan's rippling muscles and his rock-hard arm pulling her close.

"Comfy?" he asked once, speaking the word so close to Lydia's ear that his warm breath sent a shiver down her spine.

"Oh, yes," she replied, the words very nearly refusing to come out of her throat. "Quite."

Barbara sat beside them on the front-facing seat, and as usual, she and her brother were involved in a good-natured argument that required the other passengers to take sides.

Captain Danforth was not loath to do so and gave it as his opinion that the young lady was correct. "The coxswain is every bit as necessary to the winning of a boat race as is the oarsmen. Whether in a boat or on a ship, every job is important."

"See there?" Barbara said, her tone smug.

Everyone began to talk at once, and not content to let the matter rest, Bernard wrote on his notepad, enlisting Jack's support.

Anyone seeing the carriage and the animated passengers would think them all thoroughly caught up in their dispute. However, in this the viewer would be mistaken, especially since at least one of the six heard not a word.

On the last position change, Evan had slipped his arm around Lydia's waist, but once the change was made, he did not release her as before. Instead, he rested his hand just above her hip, with the tips of his strong fingers just touching her ribs, and from that moment on Lydia had been totally incapable of following what anyone said.

Of course, with everyone talking at once, a lady might be forgiven for losing her train of concentration. What bothered Lydia most, though, was the way her heart was pounding, and her almost overpowering desire to relax against Evan's chest, to rest her head upon his broad shoulder, and to feel both his arms wrapped around her, holding her close.

And who would not wish for the comfort of a pair of masculine arms? Especially after the day Lydia had endured, with Penelope Fieldhurst embarrassing every female within sight, and Miss Blakesly gazing adoringly at Sebastian, as though he were the moon and the stars all rolled into one.

As for Lydia's first meeting with her beloved in eight years, that had not gone at all the way she had planned it.

During the course of the afternoon, Sebastian had managed to anger her not once but twice, making her wonder if there might be a few facets of his character that were not as noble as Lydia had always imagined them to be. Furthermore, though he had treated her in a gentlemanly manner, honesty compelled her to admit that he had not appeared particularly bowled over by the improvements eight years had wrought in her face and figure.

Nor had he made even the smallest attempt to be alone with her. And worse yet, when *she* had finally gotten *him* alone for a few moments of private conversation, he had bored her to distraction with his endless talk of horseflesh.

Given that overwhelming list of the day's disappointments, Lydia felt she was entitled to a bit of comforting.

But comforting from Evan? At the thought, Lydia had the grace to blush.

Naturally, Sebastian was the person she *really* wished to snuggle against. Evan Trent just happened to be there; that was all. True, being so close to Evan was doing strange things to Lydia's midsection, for he seemed especially appealing today, with a slightly mysterious smile pulling at the corners of his lips and the wind ruffling his hair. Still, it was Sebastian Osborne that Lydia loved.

Wasn't it?

Ten

As it turned out, the twins remained at Trent Park all of Monday and Tuesday, but according to the message sent them by their mother, they were to be fetched Wednesday afternoon.

"But Cousin," Barbara said that balmy Wednesday morning, "this is our last day, and we may never have another such opportunity." The young lady and her brother, along with Lydia and Jack, sat in the rose garden, at a wrought-iron table laden with dishes designed to temp the early morning appetite.

"Besides," Barbara added, as if presenting an irrefutable argument, "I consider it an act of Providence that there are two boats. Surely that must mean something."

Bernard was no less enthusiastic than his sister. "Only think what fun it would be. Just like Sunday's race meet. Barbara and Jack in one boat, and you and me in the other. You females can be the coxswains while us men do the rowing."

As the adult in the group, Lydia felt she should introduce all manner of objections to the scheme; yet, the adventurer in her wanted to give in to her young cousins' importuning. After touching Jack's arm to get his attention, she wrote on his notepad, *Are you quite certain you wish to race?*

At his enthusiastic nod, Lydia gave in. *Very well, but I think you and I should be a team.*

To Bernard she said, "You and your sister take one boat, and Jack and I will take the other."

"Hey, now!" Captain Danforth said, surprising them all with his sudden appearance, "what about us seafaring types? Would you leave Evan and me out of the fun?"

Lydia had not heard Evan and his guest approach, and knowing that they were together, she turned slowly. The two men had been out for an early morning ride, obviously across muddy terrain, for their boots were liberally splattered with mud, and if their windblown hair was any indication, they had ridden hard.

At the sight of Evan, appearing more casual than she had ever seen him, with his hair mussed and his usually neat collar loosened and noticeably rumpled, Lydia felt her face grow warm. Pure foolishness, of course, for she had nothing to be embarrassed about; it was just that she had not seen Evan since their ride home from the village, when she had sat upon his lap.

The minute they had stepped inside the vestibule Sunday, the butler had given Evan a note from his steward, informing him that lightning had struck one of the sheepherder's huts, burning the place to the ground. Evan had excused himself to his guests and gone immediately to assess the damage, and for all of Monday and Tuesday he had been away from the Park, seeing to the hiring of workers for the rebuilding and thatching of the hut.

Now, as he and Captain Danforth joined the foursome, Lydia could see signs of fatigue around Evan's dark eyes, and any embarrassment she may have felt disappeared in her concern for him. "You are tired," she said.

"Only a bit," he replied quietly. "But certainly not enough to prompt me to forego a race. That is," he added, looking at Barbara and Bernard, "if you two can swim."

"Like fish," Bernard assured him.

While Evan glanced toward Lydia for confirmation of the fish analogy, Barbara gave it as her opinion that they should wear "team colors."

"And we will need a starting and a finishing line," her brother added.

"Easy enough," the captain said. "While you youngsters see to the colors, Evan and I will check out the boats for seaworthiness and devise some sort of race boundaries."

After agreeing that they should all meet at the small boat landing within the half hour, the men went off toward the river. When Barbara would have caught Jack's hand to drag him along with her and her brother on their quest for team colors, Lydia stopped her. "Jack and I will wait for you here," she said. "He and I need to plan a bit of strategy."

The seriousness of her tone informed her cousins that she was not to be gainsaid, so Barbara and Bernard left her alone with their friend and went in search of the housekeeper, who was the likeliest person to know where they might find ribbons or a bit of cloth they could shred to supply the required colors.

During the fast-paced planning of the race, Lydia had watched Jack to make certain he had followed what was being said. Understandably, the lad had missed some of it. As well, though he was usually more than happy to go along with anything the twins wished to do, as the conversation had progressed, and the men had voiced their wish to participate in the competition, Lydia had seen in Jack's eyes a noticeable diminishing of his original enthusiasm.

As soon as they were alone, Lydia said, "What is amiss? Have you decided you do not wish to race after all?"

At first Jack merely shook his head, but after a bit of prodding, he wrote briefly on his pad, the gist of his message being that because he could not hear, he was afraid he would not be able to match his strokes with those of a teammate.

"But I will be the coxswain," Lydia said, "and I will set the pace for the two of you."

"What good is a coxswain to me?" Jack said, the fact that he had spoken an indication of his frustration. "I cannot *hear!*"

Before Lydia could reply, Jack scribbled something on his notepad, then gave it to her to read. *I cannot perform as a team member. Whichever boat has me in it will be defeated.*

Lydia had not seen the lad look so dejected since before he met the twins, but she understood his doubts, and his wish not to be the cause of his team losing. No point in telling him that it did not matter who won or lost; males were too competitive to understand that particular philosophy. Instead, she gave her energy to thinking of a way that would allow Jack to become part of a team.

The answer, when it came to her, was so simple she wondered why she had not thought of it before. "I have it!" she said. "The perfect solution."

Using Jack's pad and pencil, Lydia explained her idea, and when she was finished, she asked, "What do you think?"

"I think it will work," he said, the words spoken slowly. His willingness to speak again told Lydia that he appreciated her effort, and the brightness of his eyes left her in no doubt as to how much he had wanted to be a part of the competition . . . to participate like any normal boy.

"It *will* work," Lydia assured him. "And our team will win!"

Jack had only just put away his notepad when the twins returned to the garden, waving strips torn from brightly colored cloth—three strips of red and three of green. Not content with their discovery of the cloth, they had also alerted the entire house to the impending race.

It was not surprising, therefore, that when the competitors made their way down the Italian-style terraces that gave access to the shallow tributary of the Mersey River, they found a small but vocal group of spectators waiting at the boat landing.

Lady Trent was there, seated on a slipper chair brought down from the house and placed in the shade of the thick-branched beech tree, and milling about quite close to the riverbank were eight of the house servants, including Palmer, the very proper butler, and three of the stable lads. The presence of so many humans had sent the silent swans and the not-so-silent grebes to the far shore, leaving the way clear for the boats.

Due to the unexpected holiday, everyone was in a festive mood, laughing and enjoying the sunshine, and generally looking forward to the excitement of

the race. As well, there appeared to be a relaxation
of the usual servant hierarchy, and one of the stable
lads found enough courage to inquire if Mr. Palmer
was of a mind to consider a small wager.

"How small?" Palmer asked.

"A shilling, sir. On t'captain's boat."

"The captain, you say?"

The stable lad nodded. "Righto!" Growing a bit
bolder, he added, "No doubt about it, Mr. Palmer.
T'captain'll be t'winner. 'E's not too tall to fit in
t'boat, and any bloke as 'as eyes in 'is 'ead can see
t'captain will strip to advantage. Muscles on top of
muscles, 'as t'captain."

The housekeeper, overhearing the stable lad, whispered to the cook, "A surfeit of muscles the navy
gentleman may have, but none can deny that the
master is a fine figure of a man as well."

"He is that." the cook agreed. "And I'll bet me
new bonnet his lordship's boat will win."

"And why should it not?" the affronted housekeeper wanted to know. "Lord Trent can do anything he puts his mind to. He was always a one for
giving a thing his all. Even when he was a lad.
Though that," she said with finality, "was long before *you* came to the Park."

Whatever the cook's possible rejoinder, it remained unsaid, for a general shout of welcome
greeted Evan and Captain Danforth. They had appeared from around the bend of the river, rowing
the two wide, flat-bottomed punts toward the landing.

Lydia was pleased to observe the way the two craft
sat in the water, balanced and not too low, reassuring
her that neither boat leaked to any great degree.

However, any resemblance between those two cumbersome, discolored dinosaurs and the twelve sleek shells they had watched glide across the Mersey during Sunday's race was purely coincidental.

The two gentlemen, their riding coats removed and left who-knew-where, had obviously just come from setting up the starting and finishing lines, and while they tied the punts to the landing and climbed out, Lydia took the opportunity to stroll over to the beech tree. Since everyone's attention was on the action at the landing, Lydia was able to choose just the sort of smallish, yet sturdy branch she wanted. Moving quickly, she broke off the short, straight limb, stripped it of its leaves, then tucked it beneath her arm, next to her ribs, pleased that no one had seen her.

Had she but known it, at least one person had noticed her actions. Evan had been watching her since he climbed out of the punt, and wondered why in the world a young lady would want a beech limb.

Of course, Lydia Swann was no ordinary young lady. Nor, for that matter, was she anything like her namesakes. No docile, yet decorative beauty, Lydia was too filled with the joy of living, and her nature was too adventurous for her to be likened to the quiet, elegant swan.

No, Lydia was more like the grebes, who were even now giving vocal evidence of their displeasure at having been displaced to the far riverbank.

Lydia was full of pluck, and every bit as colorful as the grebes, for at the moment her red hair shone in the sunlight like bright, new copper. As Evan watched her walk purposefully toward him, he won-

dered why he had never noticed before how warm
and vibrant red hair could be, or how it invited a
man to touch its warmth, its vitality.

"Lord Trent," Bernard Hilton said, drawing
Evan's thoughts most reluctantly from a rather
erotic daydream of himself touching Lydia's hair,
the thick, coppery tresses unbound and spilling
loosely about her shoulders, and her slender, yet
very feminine body clothed only in a translucent
night rail and . . . "Sir!" the boy said trying to get
his attention once more.

"What is it?" Evan replied, the words spoken
more sharply than was his habit. To atone for his
irritability, he placed his hand on the lad's shoulder
and asked what he could do for him.

"Choose your color," Bernard said, holding out
cloth strips: two red and one green. "Barb and I are
on the green team," he said, "and Jack and Cousin
Lydia are on the red. It wants only for you and Captain Danforth to choose your colors."

Without a word, Evan lifted the two red strips
from the boy's fingers. By that time, Lydia had arrived at the landing, so he held one of the strips
toward her. "Will you do the honors?"

When she nodded, he turned sideways and rested
his fisted hand on his hip, so that she could tie the
team color above his elbow. It was not an easy task,
for her movements were hampered by the beech
branch still concealed beneath her arm.

Lowering his voice, Evan said, "Might as well give
over, for your secret is out."

"Secret? I am certain I do not know what you
mean. I have no . . ." Her protest trailed off, for

she noticed Evan staring pointedly at the arm concealing the tree branch.

"Care to tell me, madam, why you felt the need for a weapon, especially one that necessitated denuding my beech tree?"

"Weapon? It is no such thing. And I did not denude your tree."

"Pray, do not try to deny it, for I saw you stripping the leaves from the stolen limb. And since we are to occupy the same boat, I can only hope that it was not your intention to . . . er, whip your team into shape."

Lydia chuckled. "You would be wise, my lord, not to put ideas into my head."

Evan took the second red strip, and without asking permission, lifted her arm far enough to allow him to tie on the color. For some reason, the simple act brought warmth to Lydia's cheeks. She had tied his ribbon, and now he was tying hers, and the reciprocation seemed suddenly quite intimate to her, almost like an exchanging of rings.

Exchanging of rings! With that thought, Lydia's cheeks positively burned.

What on earth had put such an idiotic notion into her head? Perhaps it was the realization only this morning that she had but six days left in which to inspire Sebastian to propose marriage. The time was running out, and Lydia had seen her beloved only once, and during that meeting she had made no progress whatever toward receiving a betrothal ring.

Sebastian's betrothal ring, she reminded herself.

Needing to put the subject of rings from her mind, she showed the beech branch to Evan. "As coxswain," she said, "it will be my job to set the pace for the oarsmen."

"Agreed," he said, the look on his face still perplexed. "And that job necessitates a tree limb because?"

"Because Jack will be unable to hear my voice. For that reason, he and I—"

"Damnation!" Evan closed his eyes as if curbing a wish to give voice to an even stronger oath. "I had not given a thought to possible difficulties for Jack." Frustrated, Evan ran his hand through his already windblown hair. "What sort of man would forget something so important?"

"An average man, I should think. Most people have to be reminded from time to time that life's race does not start out evenly for everyone involved, and that adjustments must sometimes be made to help even the odds, as it were."

"But I am his kinsman. I should have thought of something beforehand."

"Next time," Lydia said, "I feel certain you will. None of us are as perceptive about others' needs as we could be. For now, however, there is no point in chastising yourself, for Jack and I have devised a plan whereby each time I call 'Pull,' I will tap him on the back with the branch."

Evan said nothing for a moment; then he lifted Lydia's hand and pressed a kiss upon her fingers. It was a simple gesture, one any gentleman might have made, but at the feel of Evan's warm lips lingering just that extra bit longer than expected upon her flesh, a quite complex set of reactions took place inside Lydia—not the least of which was a deliciously liquid feeling that seemed to invade her bones.

Afraid her knees might give way beneath her at any second, she eased her hand from Evan's. "As you noted," she said, her voice trembling just the least little bit, "I have the stick, but I will need something to wrap around the end to soften the blows, just in case I should become too exuberant. I would not like Jack to survive the race only to be scarred for life by his team's coxswain."

"Now that is a problem I can fix." Evan's voice sounded so normal, so unaffected, that Lydia wondered how a kiss—even such a simple one—could have had such a profound effect upon the receiver and yet mean nothing to the giver.

"Will this do?" he asked, removing his cravat and holding the linen toward her.

Before she could reply, Jack joined them, his team color already tied around his arm, and his youthful face beaming with pride and anticipation. Obviously realizing the significance of the branch, he took it from Lydia and held it immobile while she wrapped the cravat around the end and tied it securely.

"I fear the linen will be ruined, Evan, for—" She said no more, for when she looked up from her task, she caught Evan staring at her, watching her tie the ends of the cravat, and the intense look in his dark eyes stirred something deep inside her.

Once again Lydia decided she must be reading more into an act than it merited, for when Evan spoke, his manner was not the least intense; in fact, his words were teasing. "I have dozens of cravats, madam, and I do not begrudge you the use of one of them. In fact, if it will aid our team, I should be happy to contribute my shirt as well."

Before Lydia could give him the set-down he deserved for having uttered such an outrageous suggestion, Bernard called, "Coxswains, are your teams ready?" his raised voice bringing a hush to competitors and spectators alike.

"Red team ready," Lydia replied.

"Green team ready," Barbara echoed.

The coxswains having spoken for the preparedness of their respective teams, all six of the participants climbed aboard their boats. Evan gave Lydia his hand to assist her to her place in the stern; then he and Jack sat side-by-side on the board seat in the center of the hull, each one manning one oar.

After a couple of the stable lads gave the punts a push off from the landing, the oarsmen rowed downriver about a quarter of a mile south of the landing. Their destination was a rope visible some six feet in the air, a rope that had been stretched across the water, strung from a willow-tree branch on the left bank of the river to a willow-tree branch on the right.

A rope had been similarly affixed upriver about a quarter mile north of the landing. Since their tributary of the Mersey did not boast a straight mile, Evan and the captain had agreed earlier that the competitors would row upstream, cross under that rope, then turn and row back downstream. The first boat to complete the mile and pass beneath the downstream rope would be the winner.

The first part of the race, being upstream, would be the most difficult, for the oarsmen would be rowing against the current, but even the trip downstream would be no easy feat. As soon as Evan and Jack manned the oars and began paddling to the starting line, it became apparent to Lydia that Evan would be obliged to adjust his stronger, deeper strokes to suit those of his younger and less-muscled cousin. If the strokes were not perfectly matched, the boat would obey the law of physics and spin round and round, turning in the direction of the stronger rower.

Because her job had not yet begun, Lydia was able to observe man and boy in action. Evan's white shirt was already damp, and as he dipped his oar into the water, then pulled, the shirt adhered to his broad back, revealing the rather awe-inspiring elasticity of his contracting muscles.

And Evan was beautifully muscled! Never mind Captain Danforth's greater bulk, Evan was grace in motion, and had Lydia not seen it for herself, she would never have known how truly beautiful a man's body could be.

She was practically mesmerized by the exhibit of splendidly fit masculinity before her, and to her embarrassment, it crossed Lydia's mind more than once that Evan might appear even more mesmerizing if he had, indeed, given her his shirt.

Lydia was wondering if the skin on his back was as sun-bronzed as that on his face, when the punt crossed beneath the rope and she was obliged to call herself to attention. Within seconds, however, the excitement of the coming race took hold of her, and she sat up very straight, the beech branch at the ready. Meanwhile, as they waited for the green team's boat to come alongside, Evan and Jack back-paddled to keep the boat from flowing even farther downstream.

The other punt arrived within seconds, and once the bows of the two boats were lined up as closely as could be expected, Barbara and Lydia nodded to each other, and the race began.

"Pull, pull!" Barbara yelled.

"Pull!" Lydia yelled, and as she yelled, she thumped Jack on the shoulder with the cravat-wrapped branch. Unfortunately, their team got off to a bad start, with Evan dipping his oar too deeply into the water and causing the punt to pull strongly to starboard. Realizing his error, he eased up, and soon the boat was headed in a relatively straight line upriver. As well, by the time the oarsmen made the correction, Lydia had mastered her own job, the call and the thump perfectly synchronized. "Pull," *thump!* "Pull," *thump!* "Pull," *thump!*

The green team had made a much smoother beginning, and for the five or six minutes required to cover the half mile upriver, they maintained a lead of several strokes. When they crossed under the upstream rope, however, there was a miscommunication as to which way they should turn, and as a result, they did not turn at all, but continued forward.

"To the right!" Barbara yelled at the top of her voice. "Turn, turn!" Then, with frustration evident in her tone, "The *other* right, Bernard!" She punctuated this order by giving her brother a resounding punch between his shoulder blades. "Let the captain do the turning!"

The boy eased up for a stroke or two, allowing Captain Danforth to execute the deeper strokes that turned the boat around. By the time they were faced downstream, however, they had forfeited their lead, for Lydia's red team had already turned their boat and begun the much easier journey downriver toward the finish line.

"Faster, greens!" someone called from the water's edge.

"You can do it, reds!" another called.

"Pull, pull!" Barbara yelled, her eagerness heightened by the shouted encouragement coming from the spectators.

No less eager than her cousin to win, Lydia was obliged to curtail her enthusiasm in order to concentrate on maintaining the perfect rhythm of the call and the thump. She, Evan, and Jack were working well as a team, and she wanted to do nothing to spoil their success.

During the final minute of the race, the green team pulled alongside the red, and the two punts glided along together for several seconds, not so much as an inch separating the points of their bows. The oarsmen of both boats dipped and pulled with all their strength. No matter how hard they tried, however, it seemed that neither team could pull ahead of the other.

"Pull! Pull!" from the green boat.

"Pull," *thump*. "Pull," *thump* from the red.

It was all Lydia could do to contain herself, to force herself to maintain the rhythm. She wanted to scream. To shout. To jump up and down. Anything to get the red team's punt ahead once again.

Then, when they were mere inches from the finish line, with no more than seconds to spare, Lydia saw the bow of the green team's punt pull out ahead. With a shout of victory, the other team crossed beneath the rope.

"Hurray!" Barbara yelled.

"We won!" her brother shouted. "We won!"

Even Captain Danforth let out a victory yell.

The red team's punt followed the winning boat across the finish line, and as Lydia heard her cousins shouting in joy over their victory, and saw them waving their arms above their heads and patting each other on the shoulders in congratulations, she knew a moment of bona fide disappointment. Almost immediately, however, she remembered the exhileration and joy of the race, and her disappointment vanished.

In every competition, only one team comes out the victor, but in truth, crossing the finish line first is but a small part of competing. Now that it was all over, Lydia knew she would never forget this experience, and similarly she would not allow any negative thoughts to rob her of the pleasure she had felt at being a part of the team.

Unfortunately, she doubted that a lad of Jack's age would share her view.

She knew how desperately the boy wanted to do all the things he had done before he lost his hearing, to prove, if only to himself, that he was still the person he had always been. And though Lydia felt that participating was what truly mattered, she could appreciate Jack's desire to win. Though dreading the look she feared she would see in the lad's eyes, she put her hands on his shoulders and urged him to turn toward her, so that she could offer whatever comfort he would allow.

When Jack turned, his face was covered in perspiration from the supreme physical effort he had made, and his breath was coming in gasps, but to

Lydia's delight, he smiled from ear to ear, and his eyes were alight with happiness.

To Lydia's further joy, while the lad struggled to fill his lungs, he closed his fist and pointed his thumb and first finger to form the letter signifying her name; then he placed the letter over his heart, holding it there for just an instant.

Lydia understood that Jack's use of that particular gesture was twofold. He was thanking her for sharing in this experience, as well as telling her that he loved her, and Lydia, too overcome with emotion to speak, made the sign for Jack's name and placed the signing fingers against her heart, to show him that she felt exactly as he did.

After a moment, the boy began to laugh. "Next time," he said, the slightly stilted words coming out in a breathy gasp, "we win."

"Right you are," Evan agreed, his smile every bit as wide as his cousin's. "I consider this to have been an excellent practice run, and next time we will show those greens how it is really done!"

"Won't we just!" Lydia concurred.

Having said this, she looked directly at Evan, and their gazes met. For what seemed a long time, neither of them looked away; then Evan, apparently as caught up in the exhileration of the moment as was his young cousin, reached out his arm, caught Lydia around the waist, and pulled her against his chest. Hesitating only a moment, he bent his head, and to Lydia's complete astonishment, he kissed her full on the lips.

Eleven

Lydia had never been so surprised in her life. Totally without warning, Evan had pulled her to him and kissed her. She had been kissed before, of course—once, when she was fourteen, by a friend's spindly legged brother—but never by a grown man, and at the moment she could not think what to do, not with Evan holding her so tightly she could feel the beat of his heart against her breast. As for the feel of his warm lips moving against hers, that particular sensation robbed her of all coherent thought.

The kiss lasted mere seconds, and when Evan lifted his head, he was no longer smiling. His thoughts, however, were apparently still on the race, for he said, "That was my way of saying 'Thank you,' to the best coxswain a team ever had."

Thank you! Gratitude was the last thing Lydia wanted!

Because she was still reeling from Evan's kiss, and the magical feel of her body being crushed against his, his words both disappointed and angered her, and she wanted nothing so much as to push away from him, to be freed from his strong embrace.

And push away she did. Unfortunately, the kiss that had robbed her of rational thought had also made her forget that she was still in a small boat, and when Evan released her, Lydia turned, thinking to run away. She took one step, caught the heel of her boot on the beech branch she had dropped, and pitched headfirst over the side of the boat.

Though surprised to be hurtling through space, Lydia was not frightened about falling into the river, for she knew herself to be a good swimmer. Even so, she was unprepared for the shock of the ice-cold water, and the instant she hit the surface, she gasped. That was her second mistake, of course, for she took in half the Mersey in one gulp.

Thankfully, at that spot, the river was not much more than seven-feet deep, so as soon as Lydia touched bottom, she got her feet beneath her, bent her knees, and pushed herself back up to the surface where she could find some air. Unfortunately, breathing was out of the question, for she was caught in a paroxysm of coughing, with muddy liquid pouring from her mouth, her nose, and her eyes.

As for treading water, a thing she did with ease in the placid pond back home, that feat was almost beyond her, due to the swiftly moving current. Furthermore, she might as well have been tied with ropes, for her legs were constricted by the yards of sodden muslin and lawn of her skirt and petticoat, and her boots were rapidly filling with water and already threatening to pull her back down.

"Lydia!" Evan shouted the instant he saw her lose her footing, and though he grabbed for her, he was not fast enough, and over the side she went. Immediately, he stood, took a quick breath, and dove in after her. By the time he surfaced, Lydia's head was above water, but she was choking, and her attempt to stay afloat was proving difficult.

"Here," he said, catching her around the waist and taking her full weight against him. "I have you."

Lydia wrapped her arms around his shoulders, allowing him to hold her while she rid herself of the water she had swallowed. She was grateful for his support, but the moment she ceased coughing, embarrassment prompted her to attempt to push away from him. "I can swim," she said.

"I know you can, but—"

Evan got no further, for Michael had pulled up his boat next to the two swimmers and was reaching for Lydia. "Give me your hands," he said. She complied instantly, allowing Michael to lift her out of the water and into his boat, where she collapsed in a heap on the floor at the rowers' feet.

Wasting no time, Evan hoisted himself into his own punt, and he and an ashen-faced Jack began rowing in earnest, following close behind Michael's boat.

The moment Evan and Jack reached the landing, Evan leaped out and ran to the other punt. With four people in his boat, Michael dared not move and upset the delicate balance, so he waited until Evan arrived before attempting to help Lydia stand. "Steady there," he said, his hands on either side of her waist. "Not too fast. I should think one swim a day would be quite enough for anyone, even as intrepid a lady as you."

As soon as Lydia was on her feet, Evan reached down for her hands and pulled her up and onto the landing. Water dripped from every inch of her clothing and her hair, which had come loose and was hanging in her face, and her thin muslin dress was plastered to her body. She was shivering like a blancmange, but when Evan would have lifted her into his arms to carry her up to the house, she stepped back.

"I am n-not injured," she said. "M-merely c-cold. And fr-frightfully embarrassed."

"You? You have nothing to be embarrassed about. I am to blame for this entire fiasco, and it is I who should be—"

"I say there," someone called from among the spectators. "Do you need a hand?"

"Sebastian," Lydia whispered through chattering teeth. "It w-wanted only that. And m-me resembling nothing so m-much as a drowned r-rat."

"If you do not wish Osborne to see you, I will—" Evan stopped, for he had taken a good look at her himself, and with the sodden muslin clinging to her body like a limpet, she might as well have been na-ked. Every line, every curve of her body was displayed, and one glance at the front of her bodice revealed . . . "Damnation!"

If she was embarrassed before, she will be mortified once she discovers that she has been so exposed.

Evan wanted to curse. To kick something, preferably himself. How could he have done this to Lydia? She was a gently reared young lady, full of energy and liveliness and more humanity than he had ever witnessed in one person. She had been a breath of fresh air in his home, sharing her joy for life with him, his mother, and Jack. And how had Evan repaid her? By mauling her about in view of her relatives and half his servants, then exposing her slender, innocent body to prying eyes.

Wanting to shield her, especially from Sebastian and his guests, Evan lowered his voice and spoke directly into Lydia's ear. "Listen to me," he said. "I want you to turn around and keep your back to the spectators. Do not move until I get my coat. And do not attempt to leave."

"W-why? What is—" Sensing what might have prompted his instructions, Lydia looked down, and what she saw made her gasp. The sprigged muslin and the lawn shift beneath it had become as transparent as tissue paper, and it was possible to see all the way to her skin. Mortified, she crossed her arms over her chest; then she turned to face the river, her back to the interested onlookers.

"Deuce take it!" she heard Evan mutter. "Where is that wretched coat?"

Lydia recalled that he had been in shirtsleeves when the race began, and she was about to remind him of that fact when he called to one of the scullery maids who stood with the other servants, all of whom stared openmouthed, watching their master and his guest as though they were part of a raree-show put on as an entertainment following the race. "You, there," Evan said. "Come over here."

The girl obeyed, though she approached slowly and dropped a nervous curtsy. "Yes, my lord?"

"Give me your apron," Evan said.

"My apron?" She stared at him, her eyes wide with disbelief, as if he had asked her to remove a foot or a hand. "But, sir, I—"

"Deuce take it, woman, give me the apron. Can you not see that Miss Swann is soaked to her skin?"

"Yes, sir—I mean, my lord."

While the frightened maid untied the strings of

her apron, then slipped her arms out, Evan called to those of his servants who stood gawking. "Anyone in my employ who is still here thirty seconds from now will find themselves looking for a new position. Do I make myself clear?"

The servants, even the oh-so-proper butler, scurried away like terrified mice. "Oh, sir," said the scullery maid, tears coursing down her face, "if you give me the sack, I've no place to go but the workhou—"

"Not you," he said. "You may remain. Just take the apron to Miss Swann. There's a good girl. Then once she is covered, return to the kitchen and tell Cook to have a pot of tea and some broth sent up to the lady's bedchamber. And see that a hot bath is prepared."

"Yes, my lord."

While Evan was sending the servants away, Lydia heard the captain tie his boat to the landing and bid Jack and Bernard come with him. Without a word to Lydia, the three males walked away, leaving Barbara there with her cousin.

"I will help her," Barbara said, taking the apron from the maid. "You may go."

"Yes, miss." The frightened servant bobbed a curtsy, then turned and ran, the sound of her hard-soled boots echoing beneath the wooden landing.

"Slip your arms through here," Barbara said, holding out the thick cotton apron. "It is none too clean, but the bib will cover your . . . your front until you reach the privacy of your bedchamber."

"Oh, Barbara," Lydia said, a catch in her voice. "Is Sebastian watching?"

"No. Lady Trent and Captain Danforth are escorting everyone up to the house."

"Everyone?"

"Yes. But do not worry, for other than Sebastian, there is only Miss Blakesly and Penelope. And I promise you, they were all much too far away to see your . . . That is . . ."

"To see my exposed bosom."

Barbara's face turned bright red, and Lydia could just imagine how embarrassing this must be for a young girl. As for herself, Lydia had never been more mortified, though much of her embarrassment was a result of Evan's reaction when he realized he could see through her dress to her skin.

She had not meant to expose herself, of course; she was not that sort of female. But since she *had* revealed such an intimate portion of her anatomy, and since Evan *had* chanced to see that portion, the least he could have done was not turn away as if too unimpressed to care. He had ogled Penelope Field-hurst's charms willingly enough last Sunday at the al fresco nuncheon. Was Lydia's bosom so pitifully thin that it merited only the one glance?

"Be you sure you want to go to t'party, miss? Her ladyship said you need not if you'd prefer to remain at t'Park."

"Not go to the squire's birthday party?" Lydia turned from the dressing table to stare at the maid. "Of course I mean to go. I have been looking forward to attending."

She watched the servant lay the freshly pressed silk evening dress across the foot of the bed. It was Lydia's favorite dress, sea-foam green, and she had brought it with her especially to wear to the party.

"Besides," she added, "it is not as if I have never embarrassed myself before. And I cannot hide here in my bedchamber until it is time for me to return to my home."

It was this last thought that had convinced Lydia she must get dressed and go to Osborne Grange, no matter what. Yesterday, after her ignominious tumble into the river, she had honored Lady Trent's request that she have a hot bath and spend the rest of the day in bed, but in so doing Lydia had missed having tea with Sebastian.

She had come to Cheshire for no other reason than to see her beloved, and so far she had spent only one afternoon in his company. And the days were speeding by. Only five days remained before she must return to Swannleigh Manor.

"I am going to the party," she said again. "So if you will be so good as to get my slippers; then come help me into my dress."

"Yes, miss."

Twenty minutes later, Lydia stood before the looking glass, examining her appearance from every angle.

"Oh, miss, you look like a fairy princess, you do."

Lydia knew she was no beauty, not like her lovely sisters, but she looked especially nice tonight, and she was honest enough to admit it. The sea-foam green silk complemented her complexion and her green eyes, and the maid had done a lovely job with her hair, arranging it in a Grecian knot from which spilled half a dozen ringlets that bounced against the back of Lydia's exposed neck and shoulders.

The bodice of the dress was cut fashionably low in front, and as Lydia took another look at her reflection, she sighed, thinking how much more stylish she would appear if at least a small amount of bosom showed above the square neckline. Of course, one could not produce bosoms out of thin air, so what was the use of repining. Still . . .

"I wish I were not so thin," she muttered. "Especially in the front."

"That be easy to fix, miss. Nothing to it."

"What do you mean, easy to fix? How?"

Lydia watched in fascination as the maid went to the chest of drawers and removed a pair of silk stockings. Taking only one of them, she stretched it out, then beginning at the toe, she rolled it into a thin, half-moon shape. "You put one under each breast," she said, "and t'stocking sort of pushes t'bosom up, adding a bit of roundness up top."

While the maid rolled the second stocking, Lydia placed the first one inside her shift, below her right breast, just for curiosity's sake.

"Here's t'other one, miss."

When the second stocking was in place, Lydia stared at herself in the looking glass. The improvement was amazing! Her bosom did not even look like hers, for the tops were as round as oranges, and they peeked provocatively over the edge of her bodice.

Not that Lydia meant to make use of a bust enhancer, of course, not even a homemade one, for she knew what her mother would say about such devices—that women who used them were no better than they should be. And yet, the enhancers did improve the line of the dress.

Truth to tell, Lydia had meant to do no more than observe the effect of the rolled stockings; she had not meant to leave them in place. Before she could remove them, however, she recalled how humiliated she had felt when Evan had turned away in boredom after viewing her minuscule bosom through the wet dress. At the recollection, some imp came to life inside her brain, urging her to make Evan Trent sorry he had done that. The imp wanted to see him take a long, slow look right now, and wish he had taken a closer look yesterday when he'd had the chance.

A giggle escaped Lydia. What harm could it do if she left the enhancers in place for a few minutes? Just until Evan saw her, and she could see the expression on his face.

"I will do it!" she muttered, and before she lost her nerve, she fastened the matching sea-foam cloak around her shoulders and crossed to the bedchamber door.

"Miss," the maid called, stopping Lydia just as her hand touched the knob. "Every so often, you'll want to lean forward and adjust 'em. Otherwise, they're like to move around a bit."

"Yes, of course," Lydia said, only half listening to the warning. "And thank you for your help."

Hearing the coach and horses pull up outside, Lydia hurried down the broad staircase to the blue drawing room where she knew that Lady Trent, the captain, and Evan waited.

The two gentlemen had taken themselves off somewhere last evening, leaving the ladies to dine alone, so Lydia had not seen Evan since her ignominious tumble into the river. She might have felt embarrassment at seeing him again, had Lady Trent not come forward, her hands outstretched, and placed a kiss on Lydia's cheek.

Her ladyship looked very elegant in a gown of rose sarcenet, while Captain Danforth appeared quite dashing in his officer's formal uniform.

As for Evan, he wore an evening coat several shades darker than Lydia's green dress, and a creamy white waistcoat and white knee breeches. The clothes fit him to perfection, accentuating the hard body beneath the fabric, and recalling the feel of that body against hers, Lydia felt her cheeks grow warm.

"My dear," Lady Trent said, "you look quite lovely. That color is most becoming."

Lydia could not decide if her ladyship referred to the pink of her face or the sea-foam green of her dress. The point was moot, though, for the captain stepped forward and made her a formal bow. "You will put the other ladies at the party to shame, Miss Swann. Do you not agree, Evan?"

Before Evan could say yeah or nay, the butler appeared at the door to inform them that John Coachman had brought the landau around.

"Very good," Evan said. He offered his arm to his mother. "Let us not keep the horses standing."

"Miss Swann," the captain said, a friendly smile upon his face. "Shall we?"

Lydia returned his smile. "We shall," she said; then she placed her hand upon his proffered arm and allowed him to escort her to the waiting carriage. Not once during the drive to Osborne Grange did Lydia spare a thought for the enhancers she had meant to remove.

Osborne Grange being an unpretentious establishment, the squire and his lady, along with the squire's sister, Mrs. Fieldhurst, greeted the guests in the vestibule. After the required half a minute of banal exchanges, the squire accepted the Trent party's best wishes for a happy birthday; then he invited the foursome to join the dancers or the card-players, whichever entertainment suited them best.

"I am for the card tables," the captain informed any who cared to know. "But if I may, Miss Swann, I will beg a dance from you after supper." He turned to Lady Trent. "And if your ladyship means to dance, pray save a gavotte for me, ma'am."

"Foolish boy," Lady Trent said, giving him a tap on the hand with her ivory fan. "A gavotte indeed. What nonsense. You may, however, take me down to supper. When that time comes, you will find me sitting with the chaperons, catching up on the latest *on-dits.*"

Turning her attention to her son, she said, "Find a servant to take our cloaks, my dear; then while I see if my friend, Mrs. Jeffreys, is here, you might show Lydia what a fine dancer you are."

Evan had been unusually quiet in the carriage, and even while he bowed in acknowledgment of his mother's request and summoned a passing footman to relieve the ladies of their cloaks, he managed to look everywhere but at Lydia. He still had not glanced her way when he offered her his arm and escorted her to the drawing room, where a trio consisting of two violinists and a cellist were playing a lively country dance.

Every piece of furniture had been removed from the room, but even so it proved a small space for dancing, allowing only a dozen or so couples to move about comfortably. As she and Evan watched the dancers, Lydia spied Sebastian immediately, for he was by far the most graceful man in the room.

He wore a coat of dark blue—the color a perfect foil for his blond good looks—and pale blue satin knee breeches, and Lydia did not think she had ever seen him appear more handsome. At the moment he was laughing at something his pretty partner had said, and with his head thrown back, he resembled nothing so much as a young Norse god.

"I see that Sebastian is otherwise engaged," Evan said, "but if you would not mind dancing with me, I will be happy to—"

The words seemed to hang in the air, for Evan had finally looked down at Lydia, and judging by the undisguised surprise on his face, he had finally noticed her new and improved bosom.

"Good God, madam! What have you done?"

Lydia had wanted to see Evan's reaction, and she had certainly been rewarded for her efforts, though perhaps not in the way she had hoped. Following his initial comment, he seemed lost for words, his face wholly unreadable. Lydia was considering the advisability of excusing herself and hurrying down the corridor to the ladies' retiring room to remove the enchancers, when Evan took her hand and led her to a set that was just forming and in need of another pair.

Before the dance, with its intricate steps and its weaving patterns, was finished, Lydia had been the temporary partner of every gentleman in the set, and to a man they had ogled her bosom—most of them doing so without the least bit of subtlety.

That is, every man except Evan had ogled her. Each time they met in the dance, his manner was more reserved, more distant, and if Lydia had not known better, she might have thought he was angry with her. No, not angry . . . furious.

Not surprisingly, the moment that dance was finished, one of the gentlemen in the set stepped forward and asked Evan if he would present him to the lovely lady.

Evan performed the introductions, of course. At a party such as this, where most of the guests lived in the neighborhood and were known to each other, he could not do otherwise. If his expression was anything to judge by, however, he would have preferred to land the plump, rather foppish gentleman a facer.

"Miss Swann," Evan said, "allow me to present Sir George Pilcher. George, my mother's guest, Miss Lydia Swann."

"Fair lady," the gentleman said, "make all my dearest dreams come true and say you will dance with me."

Lydia might have refused, had Penelope Fieldhurst not appeared as if from nowhere and linked her arm through Evan's. "Lord Trent," she crooned, "you naughty man. I have been waiting this age to dance with you."

Good manners dictated that Evan not spurn the forward minx, and once they took their places on the dance floor, there was nothing left for Lydia to do but agree to dance with Sir George. After being the object of several overlong looks from her partner, as well as most of the gentlemen in this new set, it did not take Lydia long to decide that she did not like conversing with gentlemen whose eyes never traveled any higher than her neck.

At the conclusion of the second set, she was

claimed immediately for the third, and though this popularity was a new experience for Lydia, she could not enjoy it. Even when she discovered that Sebastian was one of the set, his presence was not enough to lift her spirits. Like the other gentlemen, he was neither slow nor subtle in showing his admiration of her rounded bosom, but to Lydia's surprise, she received no pleasure from knowing her beloved had finally noticed that she was a woman.

When that set finally ended, Sebastian caught Lydia by the hand, and by using the excuse that they were "family," he stole her away from the gentleman who was attempting to secure her for the next dance. "Come," he said. "Allow me to escort you to the dining room, where the refreshment tables are set up."

"Yes, please," Lydia said. "A glass of punch would be lovely, for I am quite warm."

"And quite lovely," Sebastian said, tucking her hand in the crook of his elbow. "I never noticed before what beautiful eyes you have."

The compliment would have meant heaven and earth to Lydia if only her beloved had been looking a bit higher, and she was tempted to lower her lids and ask him if he could tell her the color of her eyes. She resisted the temptation and asked him instead if Barbara and Bernard were to join the party for supper.

"Heaven forbid!" he said. "My father would have allowed it, of course, but like my Aunt Fieldhurst, I thought the brats better off in their bedchambers. One can't have children ruining a party."

Brats! How could anyone, especially Sebastian, call the twins by such a derogatory name? They were polite, fun-loving youngsters, and their friendship with Jack proved that kindness and humanity were basic parts of their makeup. But perhaps Lydia had misinterpreted Sebastian's remark. Perhaps he was in jest. Evan and Captain Danforth called each other terrible names, and yet, they were the best of friends. Lydia sincerely hoped that was true in this instance.

"But the twins are so fond of the squire," she said, "and you must know they adore you. I can think of nothing that would give them greater pleasure than to join you in wishing your father a happy birthday."

"So they said. Fortunately, good sense prevailed, and they where relegated to their rooms, where they belong." Apparently bored with the conversation, Sebastian said no more until they reached the dining room.

He and Lydia were not the only couple seeking refreshments, and as a consequence, the area around the tables was rather crowded. "No point in both of us having our toes trod upon," Sebastian said. "You may wait for me over there." *There* was an alcove containing French windows and a pair of potted ferns, and after escorting Lydia there, Sebastian gave her hand a meaningful squeeze. "Promise me you will not let some other fellow steal you away while I am gone."

"I promise. I shall wait here, just me and the ferns."

While Sebastian made his way to the punch bowl, Lydia decided she would open one of the French windows an inch or two and let in a breath of fresh air. Having visited the Grange only once before, she was not familiar with the entire layout, and was pleasantly surprised to discover that a handsome stone terrace ran the full length of that side of the house.

Dozens of earthenware urns lined the low wall of the long terrace, and each container held large bouquets of succession-house roses. Their heavenly fragrance filled the air, playing Pied Piper to Lydia's senses and enticing her to come out and enjoy the balmy night. Unable to resist the temptation, she opened the French windows all the way and stepped outside.

The sky was a clear, dark-blue velvet, upon which was pinned a full moon that cast a soft, yellow-white glow upon the terrace and the lawn beyond. There were stars as well, thousands of them, and they appeared so close they invited a person to reach up and touch their brilliance.

Pleased that she had decided to wait here for Sebastian, in this unbelievably romantic setting, Lydia strolled over to one of the urns and stole a single rosebud from the bouquet. Thinking that if she pinned the flower in her hair, she could enjoy its fragrance for the rest of the evening, Lydia raised her arms, using her fingers to search out one of the hairpins the maid had used to secure the Grecian knot at the back of her head.

With the addition of the ringlets to the knot, the coiffeur proved to be more complicated than Lydia had suspected, and finding a pin that was not vital to the security of the arrangement was no simple task. Finally, her arms grew weary from the search, and she gave up, deciding to tuck the rose into the corner of her neckline.

She tried the left side first. As she tucked the flower into the neckline, her fingers brushed against the top of her left breast, and she marveled anew that the firm, round orb belonged to her. For some reason, the rose would not stay upright in that corner, so Lydia removed the flower, her intention to try it on the right side instead. As her fingers brushed against her right breast, however, all thoughts of the rose vanished, for Lydia made a horrible discovery. Half her bosom was missing!

Twelve

Lydia stood as if turned to stone. She would not—could not look down at her bodice, for she knew what she would find. On one side would be a plump, round, blatantly feminine orb that peeped over the edge of her neckline, and on the other side, a mere suggestion that was all but hidden beneath the fullness of her shift front.

No! It could not be. Fate could not be so cruel. Not now. Not in this beautifully romantic spot. Not with Sebastian about to join her at any minute, punch cups in hand, and admiration in his eyes.

Lydia could not let him see her like this. She was a fraud, and she might deserve to be found out, but not like this. Not one-sided!

And where on earth was the enhancer? It certainly was not beneath her bosom. The maid had told Lydia that the rolled stocking might shift. Why had she not heeded the warning?

After patting all around her ribs and her back, and discovering nothing, Lydia dropped to her knees and began searching around the bases of the rose-filled urns. While she was still on the stone floor, frantically looking for the lost enhancer, her beloved appeared in the doorway, a smile on his handsome face and a cup of strawberry punch in each hand.

"Did you lose something?"

You might well ask!

"Here," he said. "Let me put down these cups, and I will help you look for whatever is lost."

"No!"

Lydia wanted to disappear. She prayed to go up in a puff of smoke, never to be heard from again. Anything, just so long as she did not have to stand up and face Sebastian.

If she had had any sense—a fact tonight's fiasco showed to be a near impossibility—she would have removed the other enhancer before Sebastian joined her. She had been alone for several minutes, with ample opportunity to return to her natural state. But, of course, she had not thought of that simple solution.

Now, she must rise and face the consequences of her actions. And if Sebastian turned from her in disgust, it would be no more than she deserved. "Sebastian," she said, "I—"

She got no further, for her beloved had turned toward a pretty little wrought-iron table, his purpose to set down the cups of punch. Unfortunately, that turn proved disastrous, for he stepped on some foreign object and his foot slipped out from under him. He tried to save himself, but with both hands full, he was unable to maintain his balance, and he fell flat on his derriere.

To add insult to injury, the strawberry punch he had procured for himself and Lydia splashed all down the front of his coat and onto the pale blue knee breeches, the costly satin drinking thirstily of the spreading stains.

At first Sebastian seemed stunned; then after looking to see what had made him fall, he pitched the crystal cups, one after the other, against the stone floor, smashing them into slivers. "Bloody hell!" he shouted, catching up the rolled stocking and looking at it as if it were a serpent. "Where the devil did this come from?"

Lydia's throat felt as if someone were throttling her, cutting off her air supply, and before she could draw sufficient breath to confess to being the owner of the offending stocking, Sebastian swore again. "I'll find out who left this here," he said, "if I have to fire every female servant on the place."

At last Lydia managed to speak. "Fire them? Sebastian, you cannot mean it."

"I can and I do. Just look at these breeches. They are ruined."

"But to fire one of the servants, to take away their livelihood over such a trifle. You would not, you could not be so unforgiving."

"A trifle, you say? I will have you know these breeches cost me thirty guineas. Besides, a man must be master in his own house. Whoever left this abomination here must go."

"Sebastian," Lydia said, "the stocking is m—"

"Your pardon, Osborne," said a masculine voice, "but there is no need to fire anyone. The object belongs to me."

The speaker walked toward them from the far end of the terrace, but Lydia did not need to wait until he stepped into the light to recognize his voice.

"Lord Trent?" Sebastian said. "This *thing* belongs to you?"

Without vouchsafing a reply, Evan bent and took the rolled stocking from Sebastian's hand and placed it inside his waistcoat. "It is a keepsake," he said, "from a lady who shall remain nameless. A sort of good-luck charm, as it were.

"Of course, I realize it was not so lucky for you, but if you will be so good as to send me your tailor's bill for the breeches, I will make what reparation I can."

Not waiting for Sebastian's reply, Evan turned to Lydia, his hand held out to assist her to rise. "I cannot think that Mr. Osborne will wish to return to the party in his present state, so if you have had enough of the moonlight, ma'am, I will offer you my escort. I believe this is Captain Danforth's dance."

Lydia allowed Evan to take her back through the crowded dining room, but as soon as they were in the corridor, she stopped. "Oh, Evan," she said, a catch in her voice, "I have made a spectacle of myself. Again. Will you take me home, please?"

"Forgive me," he said, "but I cannot. To leave so early, before the toasts have been drunk to the squire's health, would occasion remark."

"More remark than this?"

From the moment they had left the terrace, Lydia had been holding her right arm folded across her chest, hoping to disguise her lopsided appearance from anyone who chanced to look her way. Now, however, she lowered her arm, allowing Evan to see what had happened. He did not bat an eye.

"Will you be guided by me?" he asked quietly.

Lydia nodded. "You cannot possibly do me any more harm than I have done myself."

"No? Was it not I who caused you to fall into the river yesterday?"

"That was not your fault."

"Yes," he said. "The fault was entirely mine."

When she would have protested, he placed his finger across her lips to silence her. "We would be better served to save this argument for another time. For now, I suggest you go to the ladies' retiring room where you can make such adjustments to your wardrobe as you think best."

He reached inside his waistcoat, as if to retrieve the rolled stocking, in case she should wish to make use of it again, and Lydia felt she could endure no more. Without a word, she turned and fled down the corridor, not stopping until she was inside the room set aside for the female guests. Finding the space unoccupied, she bent forward, reached inside her shift, and removed the remaining bust enhancer. Hoping never to see it again, she tossed the loathsome garment into a nearby wastebasket.

The room boasted a cheval glass, put there for the convenience of those ladies who wished a full view of themselves and their gowns. Lydia was not among their number. Her one desire, the thing she clung to for support through this never-ending evening, was that she would never be required to look at herself or this sea-foam dress again.

A noticeably less endowed Lydia joined Evan in the corridor, and together they returned to the drawing room. Lydia went directly to Lady Trent, who sat with the chaperons, and for the next hour she refused all requests to dance. Supper had still to be got through, and the interminable toasts to Squire Osborne's health endured, but as soon as she could do so, Lydia claimed the headache and asked Lady Trent if they might return to the Park.

"Of course, my dear. I see your aunt just there. While you and I thank her for a pleasant evening, Evan can have the coach brought around."

Lady Trent linked her arm through Lydia's, and as they made their way toward their hostess, Lydia spied Sebastian dancing with Miss Blakesly, who looked up at him with unallayed adoration in her eyes. Sebastian had changed his attire and was now dressed in a saffron-hued coat and cream-colored breeches, and he was, once again, quite the handsomest man in the room.

Somehow, though, the classic profile, the golden hair, the sky-blue eyes, no longer made Lydia's heart sing. Sebastian had revealed a side of himself tonight that Lydia could not love, a side she could not even like. The Greek god she had worshiped for eight years had shown himself to be less than a deity. And far, far less than a man.

"There is young Osborne, my dear. Do you wish to speak with him before we leave?"

Lydia shook her head. "I thank you, ma'am, but I am persuaded that Sebastian and I have said quite enough for one evening."

By the time John Coachman reined in the carriage horses before the entrance door at Trent Park, all four passengers were half asleep. The captain had been the most talkative of the foursome, supplying Evan with a surprisingly thorough recounting of two or three of his whist hands. "I vow," he said, "had we been playing for real stakes, I should now be as rich as Croesus."

"Or as poor as a church mouse."

The captain chuckled. "There is always that, of course."

In time, even that loquacious gentleman ran out of conversation, and all were quiet until they were inside the house, where they wished each other a good night's repose. While the captain went toward the book room, in search of a glass of brandy, Lady Trent kissed her son on the cheek, bid Lydia good night, then climbed the stairs to seek her bed.

Lydia was about to follow her hostess when Evan called to her. "A moment, please," he said, joining her at the foot of the stairs. "There is something I should like to say to you."

"Please, Evan, if you must read me a lecture, can it not wait until tomorrow?"

"No such reading was in my plans, but what I have to say can wait, if you insist."

She shook her head. "No, I do not insist. I will hear whatever is on your mind. I was unforgivably foolish this evening, and since it was you who saved me from making an even bigger fool of myself, I will not deny you the pleasure of raking me over the coals."

To her surprise, he smiled, and the slight curving of his lips made Lydia long to reach out and lay her palm against his uncompromisingly angular jaw.

"You are a madcap," he said, "and there is never

any guessing what you will do next, but you have done nothing to merit my censure."

"Then what is this about?"

His smile faded, and his countenance became serious once again. "It is about you," he said. "I know you love Sebastian, and since you have not asked my opinion of him, I will say nothing on that subject. But I pray you, Little Grebe, do not change who you are for him. Or for any man."

Little Grebe? When Evan said it, it sounded almost like an endearment. At least he had not called her a duckling.

"If a man truly loves you," he continued, "he will love all of you. Just as you are."

"Just as I am?" Lydia was too tired to pretend she did not understand him. "Bones and all?"

Evan caught her hand and held it between both of his, his warmth and his strength acting like a magnet, tugging at Lydia and making her wish she dared step just that little bit closer—close enough that he might be tempted to wrap his arms around her and hold her close. Hold her just for a minute. Just until the chaos in her brain ceased to torment her, and the confusion in her heart stopped threatening to reduce her to tears.

"Believe me," he said softly. "To the right man, those bones will be infinitely precious."

At his whispered words, all the embarrassment and disappointment Lydia had suffered that evening seemed to fade into nothingness, like a bad dream dispelled by the light. "How can you be so certain?"

"Because," he said, "I am a man, and *I* would not wish you to be anyone but who you are."

Thirteen

Dawn's grayish light was already peeking around the edges of the window hangings, and Lydia still had not fallen to sleep. Her thoughts were a whirlpool of confusion that would not allow her to rest, and the central figures swirling around in that mental eddy were Sebastian Osborne and Evan Trent. At some point during the long night, Lydia had been forced to let go of all her silly, girlish illusions about Sebastian. In truth, the man was a handsome face, with nothing of substance behind it.

For eight years Lydia had clung to the memory of Sebastian Osborne's handsome countenance, believing the feelings stirred by that memory were love. In those eight years she had never hesitated to criticize her sisters' many admirers for falling in love with the twins' beautiful faces; now she realized that her sentiments were every bit as shallow as those of the men she had criticized. How humbling to discover that males were not the only ones apt to misplace their brains when gazing upon a gorgeous exterior.

Lydia had needed but two brief meetings with Sebastian to discover his true nature. And what she saw, she did not like.

Poor Miss Blakesly. Lydia suspected that Sebastian would ultimately choose the mine owner's granddaughter and her fifteen thousand pounds, and Lydia felt sympathy for the raven-haired girl. Miss Blakesly loved Sebastian, and Sebastian loved only himself.

Lydia sighed, but not from sadness. From relief.

All her life she had been one of those fools who rushed in where angels feared to tread, and as a result she had often stumbled into unpleasant situations: polecats and rivers were but the most recent. Fortunately, those angels, or some higher power, had saved her from the worst possible situation—marriage to a man she would have come to hold in abhorrence. And for that salvation she was profoundly grateful.

The right man will love you for who you are.

Evan had said words to that effect last night, and he had been correct. But it was every bit as true that if Lydia genuinely loved a man, she would love him for who he was on the inside—in his heart and in his soul—and not for his exterior.

Sebastian Osborne might well be the handsomest man in the entire world, but he was not the only man. There were gentlemen right here in Cheshire who were superior to him in every way. Living, breathing men who loved and were loved, and some of them were quite handsome. Captain Danforth, for one. That gentleman possessed a very pleasing countenance, as well as a good character and a most congenial manner.

And, of course, there was Evan.

Lydia smiled, recalling the day she had met Evan Trent. Her first impression of him had been mixed, for at the time she had thought him a bit stiff. He had certainly been angry. And yet, the attribute that had underlain the stiffness and the anger was Evan's strength of character.

Lydia had known a bit of his history—a naval officer wounded in battle and decorated for bravery—but it was only later, when she came to know Evan, the man, that she saw the total person. Mixed into the complicated brew that was his personality were generous portions of kindness, dedication to his family, concern for the people of the estate who were dependent upon his good management, and loyalty to his friends.

Evan was also the manliest man Lydia had ever known. Upon that very pleasing thought she finally began to drift into sleep, with images of Evan floating inside her head. His sense of humor. His smile. Those mesmerizing brown eyes. The dizzying sweetness of his lips the day he had kissed her. His broad shoulders . . . his beautiful back . . . his . . .

A knock sounded at the bedchamber door, jarring Lydia awake, and she sat up straight, startled. It could not possibly be morning already. Surely she had been asleep for no more than a minute. And yet, full bright light was visible around the edges of the windows.

"Be you awake, miss?"

Lydia fell back against the pillows, her eyelids closing in hope that the maid might go away. She did not.

"Miss," she called again. "I've got your tray, and t'post has come. You've a letter."

Knowing there was no point in blaming the servant for *her* lack of sleep, Lydia gave in to the inevitable and bid the maid come in.

"There be toast and chocolate, miss," she said.

"Shall I set it on t'dressing table? Or you want I should bring it to t'bed?"

Lydia patted the coverlet beside her, and while the maid pushed aside the window hangings to let in the daylight, Lydia poured herself a cup of chocolate. Before she took even a sip, she picked up the letter, ran her finger beneath the plain black wafer, and broke the seal.

The letter was from her father. Lydia could not recall ever having received a letter from Sir Beecham before today, and as she unfolded the single sheet, she felt a sort of premonition. A letter had begun this trip to Cheshire, and it seemed fated that a letter should end it.

As always, her father got right to the point, not bothering with sentimental salutations.

Daughter,

 You promised to return to Swannleigh by the thirtieth of October, and though I know I need not remind you of the promise you made to your Sunday-school class, I will remind you of the promise you made to me—that you will return with Lord Trent's betrothal ring on your finger.

Lydia had not actually said she would return with *Evan's* ring, but at this point the distinction was unimportant, especially since she would not accept a ring from Sebastian now if he were the last man on earth.

She returned to the letter.

 If you are already wearing his lordship's ring, that is all well and good. But if you are not, and it looks

like the fellow will never come to the sticking point,
owing to some tender feeling he still cherishes for your
sister, there is good news. Clarissanne has decided not
to have the half-pay officer after all. So, she is now
free to accept Lord Trent's proposal.

Lydia felt as though she has been struck a blow,
and she let the letter drop from her fingers.

Evan married to Clarissanne? To be Lydia's
brother-in-law? Never! She could not endure such a
relationship.

But why?

The answer sprang to her mind even before the
brief question was completed. Why? For one reason,
and one reason only: because Lydia loved him. She
loved Evan Trent with all her heart and all her soul,
and for her to see him day after day and know he
was married to another would be torture.

When she had begun to love him she could not
say. Perhaps from the first moment she met him.
His good looks had surprised her, for he was unexpectedly tall and well-built, but Lydia suspected the
attraction began with the jolt to her senses caused
by the pure maleness that emanated from the man.

She had once likened Evan to the pirate in Mrs.
Widmore's latest novel, and in many ways he was
like the valiant Lord Timothy Tambour, with his
thick brown hair and his penetrating dark brown
eyes, but there the similarity ended. With or without
the eye patch, Evan Trent would never take anything
that belonged to someone else.

Especially not a woman who loved another man!

Lydia groaned. Evan still believed she was in love
with Sebastian. And why should he not? Any woman

who would make as big a fool of herself as she had done last evening must be either in love or deranged.

"Deranged," she said aloud. "For not realizing true love when I saw it."

"What's that, miss?"

Lydia had forgotten that she was not alone. Grabbing up Sir Beecham's letter, she crumpled it into a tight little ball. She could not, of course, do as her father had originally asked and hold Evan to that stupid proposal letter, but neither could she tell the man she loved that her beautiful sister was now free to accept his offer. Evan might discover the fact, but not from Lydia's lips.

Though she would like to think that if Evan knew she loved him he would return her affection, Lydia was enough of a realist to doubt that such a miracle would ever happen. Why should a wealthy viscount, a man of Evan's social standing, choose a woman like her? He deserved a lady with style and beauty, not a penniless, flat-chested hoyden with a proclivity for falling into unladylike scrapes.

But, oh, how she wished he could love her.

Memories began to flood her thoughts—warm, exciting memories of sitting on Evan's lap during the carriage ride, when she had closed her eyes against all sensations save the feel of his rippling muscles and his rock-hard arm pulling her close.

And there was the billiard lesson, when Evan had stretched both his arms along the length of hers and pressed his palms against the back of her hands, curving his fingers around her fingers. He had been so close Lydia could feel the rise and fall of his chest as he breathed, and the sensation had practically robbed her of the ability to think coherently, never mind learn to strike the cue ball accurately.

Then there was the kiss after the race. A kiss so sweet, so tender, and yet so passionate it made her long for more.

As for the tender way Evan had treated her at the party, protecting her from disgrace by claiming that the bust enhancer belonged to him, Lydia would never forget that piece of chivalry. And she would remember always those moments after the party, when he had called her 'Little Grebe' and said that *he* would not wish her to be anyone other than who she was.

Encouraged by this last recollection, Lydia decided she could not return to Swannleigh without first asking Evan exactly what he had meant by those words. If he had intended nothing more than to be kind, so be it. If, however, he had meant something more, perhaps that he could love her, then Lydia would not leave Trent Park without at least giving him an opportunity to tell her how he felt.

The decision made, she told the maid to come take the tray. "I have decided to go belowstairs to break my fast."

Some twenty minutes later, Lydia stepped through the door of the small cream-and-green morning room. Only one person sat at the table; unfortunately, it was not Evan.

Captain Danforth stood at her entrance and made her a bow. "Good morning, Miss Swann. I see that you, like me, stayed abed a bit longer than usual today."

Lydia smiled, trying to hide her disappointment at not finding Evan. "By today's standard, sir, does that make us early or late?"

"Decidedly tardy, I fear. I have seen nothing of young Jack or Lady Trent, but our host was leaving as I came down."

"Leaving!" Lydia blushed, for at her heated outburst, the captain had lifted a questioning eyebrow.

"Is there a problem? Something I can help you with, perhaps?"

Lydia shook her head. "I have something I wish to tell Evan. Did he say when he would return?"

"Unfortunately, he did not. I doubt he knew, for he meant to ride up to the sheep pasture to see how the workers are coming along with the rebuilding of the hut that was struck by lightning."

The captain pulled out a chair for her and held it while she sat. "I suggested to Evan that he wait until tomorrow to check on the workmen, but Evan is one of those fellows who never leaves a task for later, especially one he believes important."

"And is a shepherd's hut so important?" Lydia asked, her tone noticeably impatient. "Surely they use them only during the warm months, when the sheep are up in the high pastures."

"True," the captain replied, giving her another speculative look, "but sheepherders are not the only people who use the hut. More than once, it has been the refuge of some person in the area who has gotten trapped in the hills by the fog."

Lydia said no more, but when she tried to eat a few bites of the poached salmon and current bun the captain had been so kind as to fetch for her from the sideboard, she found both foods nearly impossible to swallow. She was not interested in food, not when an important question wanted asking.

Following the meal, Lydia went to the book room and selected a volume of poetry from one of the book-lined shelves, then settled into one of the large wing chairs. After an hour of holding the small leather-bound edition, however, she had done no more than stare at the first page.

"Evan," she muttered, "where are you?"

As the morning wore on, and Evan still had not come home, Lydia decided to speak with Lady Trent, to see if she knew any more than the captain about when Evan was expected to return.

"As you will discover one day, my dear," her ladyship replied in answer to the query, "men are forever going out without telling the women in their lives where they are bound or when they will return. It is all quite vexing. And should a woman berate them for their thoughtlessness, the dears will stare wide-eyed, unable to comprehend why we should be in the least interested in their comings and goings."

Evan's mother smiled to show she was not truly vexed, but when she continued, there was a hint of concern in her voice. "We had fog this morning," she said, "and if I am any judge of the matter, we will see more of it later in the day."

"How can you be sure?"

"After thirty-five years living this close to the Pennines, I have begun to sense when bad weather is on its way. Of course, my husband tried more than once to explain to me the reason why fog forms, but I still do not fully understand the phenomenon. It has something to do with calm, clear nights, when cold air flows down the hillside and gathers in the valley. When the sun comes up and warms the air, it rises and mixes with cooler air above, forming fog."

No more than Lady Trent did Lydia understand the causes of weather changes, but she remembered the conversation she had overheard between her hostess and her Aunt Minerva, about people becoming lost in the fog, and she knew a moment's fear. "Is Evan in any danger, ma'am?"

"No, of course not. My son was a sailor, and of necessity sailors learn to be very observant about the weather. He will know when it is time to come down from the hills."

Nothing was said for several moments; then Lady Trent asked if there was something particular Lydia needed from Evan.

At first Lydia shook her head. On second thought, however, she decided she could not, in all honesty, keep it secret that her sister was available to accept Evan's proposal. Preparatory to revealing this fact, she asked Lady Trent if she knew of the letter Evan had sent her father.

"Yes. I never read it, but I am aware of its contents. And a more idiotic venture I cannot recall. Which just goes to prove that even the most intelligent of men can sometimes behave like simpletons.

"And yet," she added, reaching over and patting Lydia's hand, "now I think of it, had it not been for that letter, my son and I would never have had the pleasure of knowing you."

The generous observation brought moisture to Lydia's eyes, and she knew she must reveal all—all, that is, except her father's original plan to palm her off on Evan. "I had a letter from my father today, and he informs me that my sister, Clarissanne, is not, after all, betrothed. According to Papa, she is now free to entertain other offers for her hand."

"I see," Lady Trent said slowly. "Clarissanne, you say?"

"Yes, ma'am. What I wish you to tell me is, should I inform Evan of my sister's changed circumstances? Would he want to know, do you think?"

Her ladyship answered very quickly. "No. Do not say a word to him." Then, more slowly, "I am persuaded, my dear, that my son is no longer interested in pursuing your sister. Not to put too fine a point on it, but when he sent that letter to your father, Evan was not all that committed to marriage. In fact, prior to that time, he had quite turned his face against ever marrying."

"Not ever?"

"That was what he said. He was content to have Jack as his heir and to let the lad marry some day and continue the line. Naturally, I always knew in my heart that Evan would change his mind once he met the right young lady."

"I do not understand. Why was Evan against marriage?"

While Lady Trent studied the wedding ring on her finger, nervously turning the plain gold band around and around, Lydia hurried to apologize for her impertinence. "Forgive me, ma'am. I had no right to ask such a personal question."

"Not at all, my dear. I was merely thinking how best to explain Evan's views. I am afraid they were shaped by his father, who was not a very faithful husband. I loved my husband dearly, and he loved me, too, in his own way. But he was not the sort of man to remain in the country, tending to his estate. He liked the excitement of London, and he liked the ladies."

Lydia did not know what to say, and thankfully, Lady Trent did not seem to expect her to reply.

"Because of my husband's roving eye, Evan has never been eager to wed, fearing he might repeat the pattern of his father's behavior."

"What nonsense!" Lydia said. "Granted, my experience of men is limited, but I have noticed that gentlemen who are addicted to sport and riding to hounds before they take a wife, generally pursue those same interests once they are wed. The same is true for those who imbibe to excess, and those who frequent gaming hells."

"Exactly," Lady Trent agreed. "And a man who is not licentious prior to marriage is not likely to become so afterward. Unfortunately, I could never convince Evan of that fact. Of course, when Jack lost his hearing and vowed that he would never wed, that put the responsibility back where it belonged, on Evan."

"At which time, he wrote the letter to my father, asking for Clarissanne."

"No, no," her ladyship corrected, "not her in particular. Just one of the young ladies. My son had no preference, for both your sisters are well-behaved girls with an abundance of beauty. To see them with their lovely blond hair and their pretty blue eyes is to behold a pair of angels on earth."

"Yes, ma'am," Lydia replied woodenly.

"However," Lady Trent added, a rather satisfied look on her face, "I believe my son has recently met someone—a young lady with slightly darker hair and eyes—who will suit him to perfection."

Darker hair!

The words were like a knife sunk into Lydia's heart. That hazel-eyed she-cat Penelope Fieldhurst had brown hair. Surely Evan had not formed a *tendre* for that . . . that *bosom on legs!* But then, Penelope was everything Lydia was not. Short, curvaceous, and without a freckle to her name.

While Lydia's thoughts grew more and more despondent, picturing Evan holding Penelope . . . kissing Penelope, Lady Trent had continued speaking.

"Of course, it is all most amusing, my dear, like some Greek comedy, for now that Evan has finally found the girl meant for him, my nephew has decided he will wed after all. His intended is your cousin, Miss Barbara Hilton." Her ladyship chuckled. "You will say it is nothing more than puppy love on Jack's part, but I take it as a good sign that the lad now foresees a normal life for himself."

Lydia heard very little of what her hostess said, for she was in too much pain to heed the lady's words. If Evan was in love with Penelope, then there was no point in Lydia telling him how *she* felt. Better to let him continue thinking she still had feelings for Sebastian; that way there would be less embarrassment for all concerned. Her mind made up, she stood suddenly and begged Lady Trent to excuse her.

"Certainly, my dear. Is something wrong? Are you ill?"

Grasping at the first excuse that came to her, Lydia said, "I suppose I am still tired from the birthday party last evening. I believe I will lie down for an hour or so."

"A good idea. Rest for a while. When Evan returns, I will have the maid wake you, and we will all have tea together."

Lydia mumbled something—she was not sure what—but whatever it was, she managed to escape Lady Trent's apartment and reach her own bedchamber before the tears began to spill down her cheeks.

On more than one occasion, Lydia's mother had assured her daughters that a good cry would cure most ills. In Lydia's case, however, Mrs. Swann's words had not proven true. For the better part of an hour, Lydia gave vent to copious tears, and all she got for her lachrymose indulgence was a sodden pillow and a very red nose.

Hoping some fresh air and a bit of exercise would clear her head, which was throbbing after the bout of tears, Lydia decided to take a short walk. With that objective in mind, she crossed to the chiffonier and removed the rain cloak her mother had insisted she pack, and after donning the woolen cloak, she exited her bedchamber, closing the door softly behind her. Not wanting to encounter anyone, she stole down the servants' stairs and out the door leading to the kitchen garden.

She did not, however, escape unseen, for one of the scullery maids was in the garden gathering the last of the autumn parsnips and placing them in a large willow basket. The girl stood and dropped a curtsy, then asked if there was anything she could do for her.

"Yes," Lydia replied. "You can tell me how to get

to the footpath that leads up to the hills, the one I see from my bedchamber window."

The maid blinked. "You want to go walking on a day like this? Begging your pardon, miss, but it's best not to go today. Fog'll be rolling in soon. Be here in two hours, maybe less."

"I mean to return long before that time."

"All the same, miss, best take a stroll in the rose garden instead. The fog rolls in quietlike, and them as b'aint careful can be in for a real surprise."

"Thank you for your concern," Lydia said. "I assure you, I do not mean to go far, but there is something important I need to think through."

"As you wish, miss." Knowing better than to ignore a request made by a guest of the Park, the maid pointed toward the stables. "The path be thataway."

Having done her duty, the servant dropped another curtsy, then returned to filling her basket with parsnips. "Something important," she mumbled, once the young lady was out of hearing range. "Miss'll change her mind soon enough about what's important if she gets herself fogged in on yonder hill."

Evan had been pleasantly surprised to find the hut completed and the gray-haired thatcher in the act of lashing his ladder to the side of the straw-covered cart, ready to return to his cottage just outside the village. "A good job," Evan said, dismounting the roan gelding. "You did yourself proud this time, Willem. That roof should last a good thirty years."

"A good twenty at least, think on." The grizzled

old thatcher smiled, revealing several gaps where teeth were missing. "If it don't last that long, your lordship can come to t'churchyard and dig me up, and I'll come fix it anew."

Evan laughed. "I cannot ask for a better guarantee."

Once Willem had driven away, the wheels of his cart squeaking overloud in the peaceful quiet of the hillside, Evan went inside the hut, leaving the door open to let in a bit of light, so he could inspect the place thoroughly. It was a small space, with scarcely enough room to allow four grown men to stretch out on the hard-packed earth floor, but it was as sound a structure as skilled artisans could make it. There were no amenities—no fireplace, no bed, no window—but if a person was caught in a snowstorm, the hut was there for needed shelter, the walls tight enough to keep that person from freezing.

Next time Evan came up this way, he would bring a blanket, a bottle of Cook's brambleberry wine, and a jar or two of preserved apples. Not a feast by any means, but enough to keep a stranded person from perishing.

The inspection of the inside did not require more than a minute or two, so Evan strolled outside to have a look at the newly thatched roof. With the hut only seven-feet high, inspecting the roof was not difficult. Evan merely climbed back into the saddle and rode slowly around the small structure.

Barring another lightning strike, that roof should last until *he* was a resident of the churchyard.

Satisfied that all was in order, Evan turned the gelding toward home. And not a minute too soon, for the fog was rising from the valley below, and in an unbelievably short time, there would be no way Evan could see well enough to risk riding home.

By the time he had reached the bottom of the hillside, about a quarter of an hour later, visibility had been reduced to no more than a foot in front of his face. For that reason, when the gelding's shoes made that welcome metallic *plink, plink* on the stone floor of the stables, Evan breathed a sigh of relief.

The grooms at Trent Park were too well trained to require instructions, so when the youth came to take the reins, Evan merely thanked him and dismounted. After patting the gelding on his damp neck to thank him for getting them both safely home, Evan hurried across the kitchen garden toward the house.

"Evan," Mary Trent called in greeting when her son strolled into the burgundy morning room. "Your timing is impeccable, for the tea tray should be here at any minute."

Evan crossed over to the fireplace and stretched his chilled hands toward the blaze, welcoming its warmth. "I might have known the tray was coming," he said, looking pointedly at the captain, who was ensconced in the wing chair closest to the hearth, "for Michael has that lean and hungry look."

Michael chuckled. "I do not know about the lean part, but I am certainly ready for one of Lady Trent's world-famous teas."

"World famous?" Lady Trent asked.

"Quite, dear lady, for I have spoken of them while in the far corners of the Earth. Your praises have been sung from Singapore to the Cape of Good Hope, and from Madagascar to Istanbul."

They were all three laughing at some further foolishness Michael was relating, when the butler opened the door and asked Evan if he might speak with him privately. "In the corridor, if you please, my lord."

Such an unheard-of request prompted Evan to move immediately toward the door. "What is it, Palmer?"

"It is Miss Swann," the butler said.

"Miss Swann? What about her?"

The very proper servant swallowed nervously. "Your lordship knows I am not easily rattled, and I do not wish to raise undue alarm—"

"Out with it, man! What have you to say concerning Miss Swann?"

Palmer turned quite red in the face. "We cannot find the young lady, my lord."

"Cannot find her? What nonsense is this?"

"Miss is not in her room, sir, and after a thorough search of the house, I have concluded that she is not under this roof. After conducting the search, I discovered that one of the scullery maids had seen the young lady set out for a walk fully an hour ago."

Evan let out the breath he had not realized he was holding. "There you have it, then. Miss Swann is probably in the rose garden. Chances are she was reading a book and has lost all track of time."

The butler cleared his throat. "Beg pardon, my lord, but Miss Swann did not walk in the garden. She asked the scullery maid for directions to the path that leads up the hills."

"Deuce take it! Did the girl not tell her a fog was likely?"

"She told her, sir. But Miss Swann said she would

return shortly, adding that she had some important reason for going."

Important! What the devil could be important enough to take a sane person up the hill path in this weather? Evan had no more than asked himself that question when the answer came to him. Sebastian Osborne. Osborne! "Damn his eyes!"

"Sir?" said the startled butler.

"Not you, Palmer. I was thinking of someone else."

Evan put his hand on the butler's shoulder, his purpose to enlist the man in his plans. "You are quite certain that the lady cannot be anywhere in the house?"

"Quite certain, my lord."

"Very well. Then, while I go change into walking boots, I will need you to prepare a few items for me. If Miss Swann is still on the hill, she is in more danger than she could possibly imagine."

Fourteen

Lydia had been right, a long walk was exactly what she needed. Never a sedentary person, she enjoyed a bit of daily exercise. As well, the fresh air had cleared the throbbing in her head, though it had done nothing whatever to dispel the ache in her heart.

The path up the hillside had proved much steeper and more serpentine than it had appeared from Lydia's bedchamber window, and there were places where she was obliged to walk carefully, catching hold of the limbs of stunted scrub pines and unforgiving gorse to keep from falling. Patches of grass, slippery from undried dew, cropped up from time to time, and there were unexpected drop-offs hid around every bend, just waiting to trap the unwary.

Once she had climbed halfway up the hillside, a distance of no more than a mile as the crow flies, her breathing grew labored, and she decided it would be wise to find a resting spot in which to catch her breath before she attempted the trip back down. Spying such a spot—an outcropping of boulders rubbed smooth by perhaps thousands of years of wind and rain—Lydia made her way to one particular boulder that was low enough to act as a sort of stool, with the boulder just behind it serving as an adequate, if rather unyielding, backrest.

After wrapping the fullness of her cloak around her to shield her dress from any moisture on the large rock, Lydia made herself comfortable. Her seat left much to be desired, but she doubted that anyone could fault the view. She had climbed just high enough to look down on the village of Alderbury and the pretty village church. The tall spire of the church stood like a beacon to the east of her, while to the west stretched red cliff after red cliff of the beautiful Peckforton Hills.

Unfortunately, the splendor of the scenery soon gave way to the despondency Lydia had felt ever since Lady Trent told her that Evan had finally found the girl meant for him—a young lady with slightly darker hair and eyes. Tears stung Lydia's eyes, but she vowed she would weep no more for what could not be.

What good would it do? Granted, she would make Evan a much better wife than Penelope Fieldhurst ever could—she was convinced of that fact—but if Evan loved Penelope, then that was the end to it.

Despite Lydia's resolve not to cry, the tears refused to obey. As if to mock her, they coursed down her cheeks, one after another, gaining momentum as they flowed. Unable to control the salty traitors, Lydia rested her head against the boulder at her back and surrendered to the inevitable. And in time she fell asleep.

Perhaps it was a result of the nearly sleepless night before, or maybe she merely cried herself into a stupor, whatever the cause, Lydia lost all track of time. The next thing she knew, she was jerked to attention by the sound of horse's hooves pounding on the path not a dozen yards from where she sat.

Embarrassed at having fallen asleep, Lydia stayed where she was until horse and rider had passed on by. When she finally stood and stretched, ready to begin her descent down the hillside, what she saw shocked her into immobility, making her realize that she had been gone much longer than she had intended.

To the east of her, where the village had once appeared clear and picturesque, now nothing showed but a dense blanket of fog, with just the tip of the church steeple peeking out of the mist. As for the Peckforton Hills to the west, those dramatic red cliffs had been completely obliterated.

For a moment, Lydia stood unmoving, stunned by what she saw, and rooted to the spot by the memory of Lady Trent's conversation with Aunt Minerva, the gist of it that some hikers out for an afternoon's walk had become lost in the fog.

"Lost for two days," her aunt had said, "huddled against the side of the mountain, afraid to move for fear of falling to their deaths!"

The thought of plummeting through space, through that thick, isolating gray fog, sent a chill through Lydia that caused her knees to tremble. Immediately she called herself to attention, for she knew better than to let fear control her. Fear was a dictator, and at that moment Lydia needed to be sovereign of her destiny.

Unlike those hikers, she was not lost on some gigantic mountain reaching thousands of feet into the air. She was on a simple hillside, and steep though the hillside might be, Lydia knew exactly where she was.

She had come directly up the path, deviating only once, when she walked over to the boulders. She was confident, however, that if she remained calm and kept to that path, she would eventually arrive at the stables and the kitchen garden.

Returning the way she had come sounded easy enough, and at first it was not too difficult, for she could still see the trees and the gorse that were close by. It was a stroke of ill luck that while Lydia made her way slowly down the winding path, the fog was working its way up to meet her.

"Remain calm," she said, hoping the sound of her voice would boost her spirits. Unfortunately, it had the opposite effect, for when she spoke, the words seemed to be swallowed up by the fog, only to be spit back at her so distorted she thought they had been spoken by someone else, someone some distance away.

"Hello?" she said. "Is anyone there?"

Anyone there? was all she heard. Muffled as it was by the fog, the phantomlike voice gave her gooseflesh, and she panicked. Suddenly terrified, she tried to run, and that mistake cost her dearly.

She had not gone more than a few feet when the path twisted. Since the fog was now swirling around her waist, obscuring everything below that level, Lydia could no longer see the ground and was unaware of the bend. One moment she was running, her boots occasionally slipping on a patch of wet grass, and the next moment she stepped off into space.

Luckily, she fell no more than three or four feet, into one of those drop-offs she had noticed on the

climb up the hillside, but during those few seconds
of descent, she had been filled with sheer terror.
When she finally landed, the wind was knocked out
of her, and she lay gasping for breath. Apart from
a sore shoulder, however, she seemed to be unharmed.

It could have been far worse, and Lydia was more
grateful than she could say that she was not lying
on some precipice overhanging a drop of hundreds
of feet, one from which she might at any moment
plummet to her death. What frightened her was the
knowledge that she had given in to panic and had
run. That fear prompted her to lie perfectly still for
an indeterminate length of time, listening to the silence of the fog and the loud pounding of her own
heart.

In time, when her heart slowed to something resembling its normal pace, she used her hands to feel
all around her until she had a pretty clear picture
of where she lay. Her suspicions confirmed that she
was in a small eroded basin no more than a few feet
deep, she climbed slowly back up to the path. This
time, however, she did not stand, hoping that if she
remained close to the ground, there would be less
chance of falling.

Rising only to her hands and knees, she began to
move cautiously. It was slow going, and every other
second she was obliged to stop and pull the tangle
of dress and cloak from between her knees, but at
least she was doing something positive, not cowering
in some ditch like a frightened sheep, *baaing* for
help.

Lydia was proud of herself for mastering her fear
and devising a foolproof mode of travel, but very

soon she learned that the prophecy was true about
pride going before a fall. While still on her hands
and knees, she collided with a large and unforgiving
boulder, hitting her forehead a telling blow. She was
not nearly as hardheaded as her parents had always
claimed, and the instant she challenged the boulder,
she lost. She cried out at the sudden pain; then she
collapsed onto her side and disappeared into a fog
of a different kind.

Evan thought he heard a cry shatter the silence,
but with the distortion affect of the fog, he could
not be certain from what direction the cry came.
"Lydia!" he shouted. "Can you hear me?"

There was no reply.

Evan had known better than to risk traveling the
path on horseback, so he had changed into heavy
climbing boots, donned a thick hunting jacket, and
come on foot. Across his back he had tied a blanket
roll containing a few medical supplies, should they
be needed.

In his left hand, he carried a sturdy metal-and-
glass lantern containing an argon reservoir. Of
course, in the dense fog, the light from the lamp
shone no farther than a few inches, but some illu-
mination was infinitely better than none, and perhaps Lydia might see the light and call to him.

In his right hand, Evan carried the thick red-and-
green-striped shillelagh that had belonged to his pa-
ternal grandfather. The fourth Viscount Trent had
become a bit of a legend in his lifetime, for he had
rescued at least a dozen lost souls who did not know
what a threat fog could be. When Evan was a child,

he had believed there was a bit of his grandfather's spirit residing in the colorful bent walking stick. Perhaps it was true, for more than once in the past half hour the shillelagh had saved Evan from a nasty fall.

He had taken a breath to call Lydia's name again when he stepped on something. Aiming the faint lantern light toward the object, he discovered that it was a hand—a female hand attached to a slender white arm.

Immediately Evan fell to his knees beside the unmoving cloaked form. He set down the lamp carefully, then moved aside Lydia's hood to see if he could ascertain the extent of her injuries. A few drops of blood trickled from a cut on her forehead, but otherwise she seemed unharmed. And to Evan's relief, she moaned and blinked her eyes.

"Lydia," he said, the word catching in his throat. "Can you hear me?"

"Evan?" she mumbled. Then, more strongly, "Evan, is it really you?"

Evan exhaled loudly. The relief of finding Lydia alive all but depleted his air supply, but after taking a fortifying breath, he caught her hand and brought it to his face. "In the flesh," he replied in answer to her question. "Feel for yourself."

She did more than feel his face, she ran her hand around to the back of his head, entwined her fingers in his hair, and held on as though to a lifeline. "You are real," she said, her voice quivering noticeably. "Thank Heaven. And thank you for coming after me. I was quite frightened."

The confession was almost Evan's undoing, and it was all he could do not to gather her in his arms and crush her against his heart, to hold her and

cover her lips with his own. To stop himself from
acting upon his dearest wishes, he said, "You, frightened? I cannot credit it."

"I was terrified for a time," she said. "But no
more. Now that you are here, I feel my resolve returning."

To hide the searing effect of her words upon his
soul, he said, "I wonder you can feel anything, for
your hands are like ice."

"I am cold," she admitted.

"Were you knocked unconscious?"

"I cannot say. All I know for certain is that I challenged a boulder, and the boulder won."

Evan smiled, admiring the pluck revealed by that
bit of humor. Hers was such a brave spirit. "A boulder was it? That explains the cut on your forehead."

When she would have reached up to the wound,
Evan stayed her hand. "Do not touch it. I have
brought bandages, and as soon as I get you to shelter, I will see what needs to be done. Can you walk?"

"To Trent Park?"

"No. I will not test your resolve for that great a
distance. The shepherd's hut is much closer, and it
is uphill. In my experience, should a person stum-
ble, it has less dramatic consequences if that person
is walking uphill."

"I can walk," she said.

Evan helped her to sit up; then he stood and
helped her to her feet. "Allow me to go first," he
said. "I will hold your hand if that is your wish, but
not to put too fine a point on it, we will both be
safer if you hold onto the rolled blanket tied to my
back. That way, my arms will be free, and I can con-

tinue to employ both the lantern and my walking stick.

"I will hold the blanket," Lydia said. "You must do what you think is best, for if you are safe, I know I will be."

Lydia had spoken the truth, but it still cost her dearly to let go of Evan's hand. As long as she touched him, she felt that nothing could harm her. It was a foolish notion, of course, for Evan was a man like any other—made of flesh-and-blood—and not indestructible. Still, while she touched him— while she could feel his warmth and his strength— she was not afraid.

When she had heard Evan call her name, and had opened her eyes to see him bending over her, it had been all she could do not to throw herself into his arms. To cling to him and beg him to hold her close and never let her go. Thankfully, before she could embarrass herself and him, she had remembered that he loved Penelope Fieldhurst.

And yet, he had risked his life to come through the fog to search for Lydia. He must care a little for her. Not enough, of course. Not nearly enough when she loved him with all her heart.

"I almost forgot," he said. "Where is Osborne? Did he leave?"

"Sebastian? I have no idea where he might be. Why should I?"

"He did meet you here, did he not?"

"No. I have not seen him since last evening."

"But I thought—" Whatever Evan thought, he decided to keep it to himself, and as soon as Lydia took hold of the blanket roll, he began to walk slowly up the path.

* * *

The hut was smaller than Lydia had expected, but in her entire life she had never been so grateful to be inside, out of the elements. With the door closed behind them, shutting the light-swallowing fog outside, the glow from the lantern increased threefold, and Lydia was able to see Evan fully for the first time. Like her, his face and hair were damp, and in addition his chin was shadowed with stubble, but for all she searched her mind, Lydia could not recall ever having seen a handsomer man.

The hut was empty, boasting not so much as a milking stool, so Evan bent on one knee, then took the blanket off his back and set it on the packed-earth floor. When he unrolled the thick woolen blanket, Lydia saw a bottle of wine, a partial loaf of bread, a pot of salve, a roll of bandages, and a small blue vial she suspected contained laudanum. She wanted no part of the laudanum, but at the sight of the bread, her stomach growled, reminding her that she had eaten only a bite or two of food since early this morning.

"Yum," she said. "Food."

Evan patted the blanket. "Sit here, and let me see what I can do for that cut. As soon as I am finished, we will have an al fresco supper."

"In this instance," Lydia said, "I believe 'al hut-o' would be a more apt description."

Evan laughed, and Lydia thought she had never heard a lovelier sound. "I like your laugh," she said. "I always have. It is so totally masculine."

At first she thought he meant not to answer, but she was mistaken. "And I like yours," he said, the words so soft she almost did not hear them. "But," he added, rather abruptly, "that cut still needs attention."

He held up his hand to help her down onto the blanket, and once she was seated, he applied salve to the cut, placed a folded bandage over it, then wound another strip of the cloth around her head to hold the bandage in place. His gentle ministrations left Lydia tingling all over, and while he tied the cloth into a knot, she said, "For such a strong man, you have a surprisingly gentle touch."

"I would never hurt you," Evan said, his voice unexpectedly husky.

That huskiness did something to Lydia's insides, making them feel all warm and fluttery, and before she realized what she was doing, she had caught Evan's hand and brought it to her lips. His skin was warm, and just the least bit rough, and for several moments Lydia buried her face in his palm. When he did not pull away, or tell her to desist, she placed a kiss where her face had been; then, unable to stop herself, she placed kiss after kiss in his palm and up and down each of his fingers. At last, she pushed aside the cuff of his sleeve and pressed her lips against the inside of his hard, thick wrist.

"Evan," she whispered against his skin, and when she looked up at him, Evan gasped.

In all his thirty years, Evan Trent had never ached so to take a woman in his arms. He longed to kiss her until she was breathless. To make love to her until she vowed she was his for eternity. Every inch of his body throbbed, and it had taken more strength than he knew he possessed to remain still while Lydia covered his hand with those sweet, sweet kisses.

When she looked up at him, her fern-green eyes were wide with innocence mixed with a promise of awakening passion, and as she stared at him, Evan died a little inside. His throat closed, hard and tight, aching with the force of what he wanted to say to her but dared not: He loved her. Loved her as he had never loved anything or anyone in his entire life. He loved her tantalizing mouth, her beautiful eyes, her silky skin, and her fiery hair. But most of all, he loved her soul, her spirit, the very life force within her.

"Evan," she whispered shyly, "you kissed me once before, in the boat. Will you kiss me again? This one last time. Please?"

Evan heard a moan, and even before he realized the sound had come from him, he had caught Lydia in his arms and was crushing her to him, kissing her face, her eyes, her neck, and finally her lips. He had never known that a mouth could taste so sweet, or that a single kiss could ignite such longing inside him.

As he continued to kiss her, her arms slipped around his neck. Heaven help him, but she fit perfectly in his arms, as though he and she had been fashioned for each other, and as she pressed herself even closer against him, her small, firm breasts imprinted themselves on his chest and on what remained of his fevered brain.

He kissed her again and again, and as he pulled her even closer, molding every inch of her slender softness to the length of him, he eased their bodies down onto the blanket.

"Evan," she murmured against his lips, and at the sound of her voice, a glimmer of sanity returned to him.

What the hell was he doing?

Foolish question! He knew exactly what he was doing! He was within an alm's ace of seducing Lydia. He knew this for a fact, though he was not at all certain she knew that was where their kisses were leading. After all, she was an innocent—an innocent in love with another man.

"Damnation," he muttered, pulling away from her.

The woman he loved was in love with Sebastian Osborne, and in all probability, what Lydia was feeling for Evan at that moment was nothing more than gratitude to him for having rescued her from the peril of the fog.

Devil take it! Gratitude was the last thing he wanted from her! He wanted *her*—all of her, body and soul—and he loved her too much to take anything less.

"Lydia," he said, his voice so ragged he barely recognized it as his, "we cannot do this. You do not know what you are doing, and I—" He swore again. "I just cannot do it."

She had been looking at him, confusion in her eyes, but now she lowered her head, hiding her face from his view. "I know," she said. "I am sorry, Evan."

Evan stood and put as much space as possible between him and the temptation of that bowed head, those softly rounded shoulders, that beguiling body. "Do not be sorry," he said. "If anyone should apologize, it is me. You were vulnerable, and I took advantage."

"No," she said, "you did not, and I will not have you blaming yourself for something I started. The fault is entirely mine."

Evan could not believe it. Lydia—sweet, naive Lydia—thought she was to blame for him nearly ravishing her. If he were not in so much pain, Evan would have laughed at the irony of the situation.

"For the sake of argument," he said, "let us agree to disagree on the subject of who is at fault."

"But—"

"And in the meantime," he added, "I have not forgotten that you took a rather serious knock on the head. You need to rest. And since we are going to be here for what may amount to ten or twelve hours, I suggest you wrap yourself in that blanket and see if you can get some sleep."

"But what of you? There is only the one blanket. Surely we can share—"

"No! We cannot share it."

Remembering the wine, Evan asked her if she wanted a swallow or two. When she declined, he put the bottle under his arm, then lifted the lamp from the floor. "I am going outside for a breath of air."

"Outside?" she said, her eyes wide as if with fear. "Please, do not go. Do not leave me here alone."

Before Evan gave in to that entreaty, he reached for the leather latch and opened the door. "I will be just on the other side of the door," he said. "If you become frightened, just call my name. I will hear you. Now, do as I asked—cover yourself and go to sleep."

Fifteen

Lydia had finally fallen asleep on the hard floor of the hut, and by the time she awoke, the morning sun had burned off most of the fog. Evan had spent the night outside the hut—probably afraid she would throw herself at him again and beg him to kiss her—and as soon as travel was possible, he had knocked on the door and told her it was time they started back down the hillside.

At some time during the night he had obviously finished off the bottle of wine, for he appeared bleary-eyed this morning and a bit worse for wear. His cheeks and chin were now covered in dark stubble—stubble that made a scraping sound when he rubbed his face; even so, Lydia longed to have him take her in his arms and kiss her as he had done last night.

I am pathetic!

Naturally, Evan did not kiss her, and though Lydia had not really expected him to do so, the fact that he did not left an ache in her heart—an ache so intense it made it difficult for her to breathe.

Silently he rolled the medicines and bandages into the blanket and set the roll against the wall of the hut for the next person who sought shelter there. Aside from asking Lydia if she was ready to go, he said no more, and during the entire journey down the path, his conversation consisted of nothing but repeated warnings for her to watch her step.

In less than half an hour they saw the Trent Park stables. When they reached the grit-stone building, Evan decided to stop off there for some unexplained reason, but before he left Lydia to return to the house by herself, he asked her if she would do something for him.

Her heartbeat quickened. "Of course. Anything. You have only to ask."

"Will you show me how to say my name?"

That was not at all what she had expected, and she was obliged to hide her disappointment. Lifting her right hand, she pointed her three fingers toward the left. "This is your initial. As I told you once before, a person may choose the way they sign their own name, so you might want to touch the three fingers to your forehead. Of course, that is only a suggestion."

As if to show his approval, he made the sign for his initial, then touched the three fingers to his forehead. "Evan," he said.

"Evan," she repeated.

"By the way," he added, softly, "did I ever thank you for all you did to ease Jack's acceptance of his hearing loss?"

"Please," Lydia said, her voice catching in her throat, "do not." Not certain she could stand much more of being with Evan and not being able to touch him, Lydia turned and ran toward the house. The moment she entered through the rear door, she found Lady Trent sitting on a small, lacquered bench in the corridor, apparently waiting for her.

"My dear child," she said, hugging Lydia to her bosom. "You cannot know how worried I was."

"Forgive me. I did not mean to—"

"No, no. Say no more. It is over and you are home."

Home. Lydia felt tears sting her eyes. Trent Park would never be her home. Evan did not love her, and in exactly two days she would return to Swannleigh, probably never to leave it again. She would never marry, she knew that now, for how could she wed another man when her heart belonged completely and irrevocably to Evan?

Lady Trent noticed the tears and hugged Lydia again. "Do not cry," she bid her. "The worst is over, and you have nothing more to fear."

No, nothing to fear. Nothing except a lifetime of loving a man I can never have.

"Come," her hostess said. "A hip bath is waiting for you in your bedchamber, and I have instructed Cook to send up a tray, for I am persuaded you must be famished. Once you are clean and fed, I promise you, you will forget all about last night's ordeal."

Lydia did not disabuse her of that conviction, instead she allowed the lady to escort her to her bedchamber where the maid was waiting to help her disrobe. Later, while Lydia sat beneath the covers, her hair brushed and pulled back with a ribbon, and a hot brick at her feet, Lady Trent returned to see how she was fairing.

"I am well, ma'am. Clean, fed, and warm. I wish you will not worry about me anymore."

"No, I will not, for I see that you and Evan are two of a kind, stoics to the end."

"He is here then, in his room?"

"Not at all. After a quick bath and a shave, he had his curricle brought around. According to my son, he had urgent business at Osborne Grange."

Urgent business. With Penelope Fieldhurst, no doubt.

As if coming to a decision, Lydia said, "Ma'am, I should like to return to Swannleigh. Would you be so kind as to arrange with the coachman to take me home today."

"Today! But, my dear, I thought you were to remain with us for at least two more days." She hesitated for a moment, but it was clear she had something more she wanted to say. "Besides, I have given the matter a great deal of thought, and I am persuaded that you and my son should announce your engagement right away."

"Engagement! No, ma'am, that is out of the question."

"But, my dear, the two of you were alone all of last night. I know your parents will agree that a wedding must take place."

But not between Evan and me. Evan loved Penelope, and Lydia wanted no part of an unwilling groom. "I appreciate your concern for my reputation, ma'am, but I am a woman grown, and I do not wish to be engaged. Not now. Not ever. What I do wish is to return to my home. Right away."

"No! You cannot do that." Lady Trent rushed to Lydia's side and took both her hands. "I should not have spoken. I thought merely to speed things along, and it seems I have made a muddle of them instead. Forgive me. Perhaps I misread the situation, but I thought you loved my son."

Lydia did not have the heart to deny it. "I-I do love him, but—"

"Say no more. I have interfered enough, as I am persuaded my son will tell me in no uncertain terms. But, please, my dear, do not go just yet."

"I-I must. I beg of you, ma'am, do not ask me to stay."

"No, not if you should dislike it. But, please, just wait until Evan returns. I know he will be able to convince you to stay."

That was what Lydia was afraid of. "Forgive me, ma'am, but I cannot wait."

Evan clicked to the grays, urging them to a trot. They had already passed through Alderbury, with its half-timbered shops and cottages, and with any luck Evan would reach Osborne Grange within the hour. It was imperative that he speak with Sebastian. Lydia was a guest at Trent Park, and as such, she was under Evan's protection. He felt it his duty to protect her.

With her protection in mind, Evan had determined to ask Sebastian point-blank about his intentions. Did he mean to marry Lydia? Or was he merely beguiling a month at home with a bit of flirtation?

"Do you love her?" he said, practicing the questions he would ask. "Is your ultimate goal matrimony? May I punch you in the nose until I mess up that handsome face?"

Evan doubted the wisdom of that last query, but if he did not like the answers to his first two questions, that third one was a given. Only let Sebastian Osborne so much as smirk, and Evan was ready to rearrange that classic profile.

Time seemed to drag as he passed one display

after another of autumn's vivid colors, the reds, the bright golds, the brilliant oranges, and at last he turned in at the Grange. As he pulled up at the entrance, he was preparing his request to speak privately with Sebastian when the door opened and Bernard Hilton came bounding out.

"Lord Trent," the boy said. "Good day, sir. I had hoped . . . That is, I thought perhaps you might be my stepbrother."

"Sebastian? Never tell me he is not here."

The lad stuffed his hands in his jacket pockets, obviously wishing he had not spoken.

"Come on," Evan said. "Out with it, lad. Has something happened to Sebastian?"

"Not exactly. It is just—" He cleared his throat. "If I tell you something, sir, may I count on your discretion?"

At Evan's nod, Bernard looked over his shoulder to make certain he would not be overheard. "Papa James found a note," he said. "Sebastian and Miss Blakesly have run off to Gretna Green."

"Palmer!" Evan called the moment he reached Trent Park. "Is my mother in the morning room?"

"Yes, my lord, but—"

"And Miss Swann, is she there as well?"

He was halfway down the corridor when the butler's words stopped him. "Miss has returned to her home, my lord. Not fifteen minutes ago."

"What?"

"It is true," Lady Trent said, hurrying to her son's side. "I tried to get her to remain, but she was adamant about leaving today. I had hoped you would return before she left, so you might convince her to stay, but—" She paused; then taking her son's arm she pulled him into the morning room, where Captain Danforth stood near a walnut vitrine, examining a pair of Sevres shepherdesses.

The moment the door was shut behind them, Lady Trent said, "Forgive me, my boy, for I am about to ask you an impertinent question, and what I reveal to you next requires that you answer me truthfully. Do you love Lydia?"

"Of course he does," the captain replied.

Evan gave his friend a speaking glance before returning his attention to his mother. "I do love her," he said. "I cannot begin to tell you how much."

"Do not even try, for time is wasting. If you love her, then go after her this minute. Kidnap her if you must, but bring her back."

"There is something I must tell her first. It seems that Sebastian Osborne has eloped with Miss Blakesly, and I fear the news will break Lydia's heart."

Mary Trent shook her head. "You are mistaken. I know this to be true, for I had it from Lydia's own lips. She no longer loves Sebastian. In fact, she knows now that her feelings for him were nothing more than a young girl's fantasy."

"Stands to reason," the captain said. "I'll grant you the fellow is devilishly good-looking, but no thinking adult could be in his presence above a half hour and still feel the least admiration for him. He hasn't a thought in his head save his own comfort."

Evan heard very little of his friend's appraisal, for his thoughts were someplace else entirely. *If Lydia no longer loves Sebastian, perhaps there is a chance she might come to love me.*

Deciding he had no alternative but to put his fate to the test, he said, "What was the name of that pirate?"

"Pirate?" his mother replied. "My boy, are you feeling quite the thing?"

"I feel wonderful, ma'am, but also just a bit nervous." He looked around him, as if searching for something. "I need an eye patch."

"Why?" the captain asked. "Is something wrong with your eye?"

"No," Lady Trent answered, "only his heart. And the young lady who fills it is a very romantic miss who admires the exploits of fictional pirates."

Evan smiled. "You told me to kidnap her if I had to, ma'am, and if I am to act the part of a brigand, I cannot do so dressed as I am."

His mother laughed aloud. "Of course you cannot. If you would emulate Lord Timothy Tambour, you must dress the part."

She looked at her son, who was immaculately attired in a Devonshire brown coat and cedar-green breeches, his neckcloth beautifully arranged. "The breeches will do, but I think the coat must go. With pirates, shirtsleeves are de rigueur."

"And no cravat," the captain said. "In novels, pirates invariably expose a bit of their manly chests."

Evan did not want to know how his friend came by that particular bit of information, but he took his advice all the same. "Shirtsleeves it is, and no cravat."

"I expect you will want a black hat and black top boots."

"Without question, ma'am."

"And I should think a dark cloak," Captain Danforth suggested, "with a collar high enough to help conceal your identity. Nothing more romantic than a partially concealed face."

"I am in possession of such a cloak," Evan assured him, "but what of the eye patch?"

His mother pondered the matter for a moment; then she smiled. "Will a half-mask do?"

Evan went to her and caught her in a bear hug, lifting her off the floor and swinging her around in one complete circle. "Madam, you are a genius."

"Put me down, you impudent rascal. Save the swashbuckling behavior for someone who will appreciate it. Believe me, I do not."

After kissing his mother's powdered cheek, Evan released her and ran from the room, his destination his bedchamber. While he transformed himself into a pirate, his friend requested the butler send word to the stables to saddle his lordship's swiftest horse. As for Lady Trent, she went immediately to the attic, where there were two trunks literally filled to overflowing with costumes of all kinds. There were silks, satins, gauzes, and even one suit of simulated armor, along with plumed hats, daggers encrusted with glass jewels, and—Heaven be praised—assorted masks.

Her ladyship found exactly what she sought, a gentleman's black leather half-mask. The eyes of the mask were cut out to allow the wearer to see clearly, while the leather covered enough of the wearer's forehead and cheeks to ensure that *he* was not seen at all clearly.

In less than ten minutes, Evan bounded down the

stairs, every inch the pirate in his swirling cloak and his black felt hat. "Perfect," he said when his mother handed him the mask. "The very thing."

On Lady Trent's instruction, John Coachman had kept the team to a crawl, a fact that enabled Evan to overtake the barouche just on the other side of the village. Naturally, the coachman recognized the white horse immediately, and taking into account the fact that only one man could handle that horse, and that man Lord Trent, the driver had no trouble guessing the identity of the masked rider. "Quality," he muttered to the groom who sat on the box beside him. "What will they think of next?"

Though the two servants were privy to the coming drama, not so Lydia Swann. When the passenger heard the report of the pistol, and felt the barouche coming to a halt, she knew a moment's apprehension. *Ye gods! A holdup here on a country road in Cheshire, in broad daylight? Has the world come to an end?*

Lydia watched the tall masked rider dismount and come to the coach. Without a word, he snatched open the door and motioned for her to get out of the vehicle. To Lydia's surprise, he offered her his hand, assisting her in a most gentlemanly manner to climb down. When she was standing beside him, however, the highwayman used the pistol he carried to motion for her to start walking toward a wooded glade off to the right.

Lydia had expected the driver and groom to come along as well, but when she looked behind her, the two men still sat on the box, their hands raised in the air. Remarkably, neither man showed the least sign of fear, and if anything, Lydia thought she detected the hint of a smile on the groom's face.

Suspecting all might not be as it seemed, she turned again to the highwayman. "If you are after money or jewels, allow me to inform you that I have neither."

The masked man merely grunted and motioned for her to keep walking. She had not gone far when she heard the crack of the coachman's whip and the immediate rattle of harness. The horses took off, but they did not gallop away at breakneck speed as one might expect. Instead, they turned and headed back in the direction of Alderbury, their pace at best a trot.

At that moment, Lydia suspected she knew how a sinking ship felt when the rats deserted it, except that one of the rats looked back, his hand over his mouth to cover his laughter.

More and more convinced that something was afoot, Lydia stopped suddenly and turned, causing the highwayman to bump into her. Politely, he caught her arm to steady her, lest she fall. "Your pardon," he muttered, his voice pitched unnaturally deep to disguise it.

He might just as well have saved himself the trouble, for Lydia knew immediately whose face was behind the mask. The moment his hand touched her arm, she knew it was Evan. In her entire life, no man save Evan had ever stirred her senses with but a simple touch. Even if he had not touched her, the game would have been up, for with him so close to her, Lydia had smelled his spicy shave soap and recognized it as the kind Evan used.

It was clear that Evan had come to stop her from

returning to her home. But why? What did he hope to gain?

Deciding to go along with the hoax until she discovered what was afoot, she said, "Sir, I have told you that I have no money or jewels. What more can you want?"

" 'Tis you I want, me beauty."

Though he had said it in that disguised voice, Lydia felt a thrill of hope shimmer along her spine.

They had reached the wooded glade, where a shallow streamed flowed quietly over a bed of smooth white rocks. Someone, perhaps a pair of lovers, had built a large campfire near the bank, but the fire had not burned long, for the wood was still stacked and usable.

In the distance, Lydia noticed a small crofter's cottage, a thin trail of smoke coming from the chimney. It reminded her of the shepherd's hut she had slept in last night, and thoughts of the hut brought memories of the kisses she and Evan had shared.

"You say you want me," she said. "For how long? Just until you tire of me?"

"I will never tire of you," Evan said.

Her question had taken him by surprise, and Evan had very nearly answered in his own voice. The trouble was, he had spoken from his heart, for should he live to be a hundred, he would never grow tired of Lydia.

There was so much he wanted to know about her. Her hopes . . . her dreams—the dreams she guarded deep inside her heart, dreams so private she had never shared them with another soul. He longed to know as well the things that intrigued the mind beneath that beautiful coppery hair.

And should he be so fortunate, Evan hoped one day his beloved would share other things with him as well. What made her sad. What brought her joy. How she liked to be held. How she liked to be kissed. All these things Evan wanted to know. Some of them he longed to discover for himself, while others he hoped she would tell him during those quiet, intimate moments that only a man and a woman who truly love each other can share.

But first he had to know if she had, indeed, put Sebastian from her heart. And, if she had, did she—could she—love Evan as he loved her?

Hesitant to put that final question to the test, he delayed the inevitable by tying the horse's reins to the limb of a small oak tree. As he turned and began to walk toward Lydia, he noticed she was staring directly at him, all the while brushing a lock of hair from her forehead.

When Evan drew closer, he realized his mistake, for she was not brushing hair from her forehead, far from it. Her thumb and little finger were folded out of sight, leaving only the three fingers visible and pointed toward her left.

While Evan stood very still, watching her, not daring to hope that she was, indeed, signing his name, Lydia touched the three fingers to her forehead, then she slowly brought them down and laid them against her heart, holding them quite still, so there was no mistaking her meaning.

Unable to find the words to tell her how happy she had made him, Evan raised his hand where she could see it, made the sign for Lydia, then pressed the sign to his heart.

Without a word, Lydia walked directly to him and

slipped her arms beneath the cloak and around his waist. After insinuating herself so close to him that Evan could feel the imprint of her delicate ribs, she turned her face up to his for a kiss.

Only too happy to oblige, Evan lowered his head, covering her mouth with his. One kiss became two, then three, then a dozen, with each successive kiss starting before the previous kiss had come to an end. Each kiss was sweeter than the one before it, so sweet Evan thought he would go insane with wanting her. Finally, all too aware that if they continued in this manner much longer, he would lose his head completely and want to lower Lydia to the ground and make love to her, Evan put his hands on her shoulders and pushed her gently away.

When she looked up at him, her eyes were questioning, and the uncertainty in her face nearly broke his heart. "We must stop, my love, while I still have a semblance of willpower. I am not, after all, that pirate, Lord Tambourine, and I do not seduce innocent maidens."

"Lord Tambour," she corrected, removing his hat and tossing it to the ground. "Besides, I like pirates."

"You do?"

"I do. Furthermore," she added, unfastening his cloak and letting it follow the hat, "if seducing is half as good as kissing, I am persuaded I would like it prodigiously."

Happier than he had ever thought possible, Evan reached up and removed the leather that obscured his face. The mask was still in his hands when Lydia twined her arms around his neck and pulled his face back down to hers. Once Evan had kissed her as much as a mere mortal could stand, he lifted his head long enough to tell her that he adored her.

"And I adore you," she said.

"Then you will marry me as soon as it can be arranged?"

"Even sooner, my handsome pirate, for I love you and I want nothing so much as to be yours forever."

Unable to remember why he had stopped kissing her, Evan took her in his arms and claimed her sweet lips once again. And Lydia, like any sensible captive, returned her beloved's kisses and bid him let the seduction begin.

ABOUT THE AUTHOR

Martha Kirkland lives with her family in Georgia. She is the author of seven Zebra Regency romances and also writes Regencies for Signet. Martha loves to hear from readers, and you may write to her c/o Zebra Books. Please include a self-addressed stamped envelope if you wish a reply.

BOOK YOUR PLACE ON OUR WEBSITE AND MAKE THE READING CONNECTION!

We've created a customized website just for our very special readers, where you can get the inside scoop on everything that's going on with Zebra, Pinnacle and Kensington books.

When you come online, you'll have the exciting opportunity to:

- View covers of upcoming books
- Read sample chapters
- Learn about our future publishing schedule (listed by publication month *and author*)
- Find out when your favorite authors will be visiting a city near you
- Search for and order backlist books from our online catalog
- Check out author bios and background information
- Send e-mail to your favorite authors
- Meet the Kensington staff online
- Join us in weekly chats with authors, readers and other guests
- Get writing guidelines
- AND MUCH MORE!

**Visit our website at
http://www.zebrabooks.com**

Celebrate Romance With Two of Today's Hottest Authors

Meagan McKinney

__In the Dark	$6.99US/$8.99CAN	0-8217-6341-5
__The Fortune Hunter	$6.50US/$8.00CAN	0-8217-6037-8
__Gentle from the Night	$5.99US/$7.50CAN	0-8217-5803-9
__A Man to Slay Dragons	$5.99US/$6.99CAN	0-8217-5345-2
__My Wicked Enchantress	$5.99US/$7.50CAN	0-8217-5661-3
__No Choice But Surrender	$5.99US/$7.50CAN	0-8217-5859-4

Meryl Sawyer

__Thunder Island	$6.99US/$8.99CAN	0-8217-6378-4
__Half Moon Bay	$6.50US/$8.00CAN	0-8217-6144-7
__The Hideaway	$5.99US/$7.50CAN	0-8217-5780-6
__Tempting Fate	$6.50US/$8.00CAN	0-8217-5858-6
__Unforgettable	$6.50US/$8.00CAN	0-8217-5564-1
